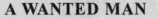
A WANTED MAN

Nate was so focused on freeing the powder keg that movement in the corral registered belatedly. Letting go, he twisted just as a heavy form pounced. Hands seized his arms and other hands seized his neck. There were two of them, and they had been waiting for him. Traggard's men were smarter than he had given them credit for being, and now they had him. Or thought they did.

"Don't struggle and we won't hurt you, mister," one said. "We're to take you alive."

If that was supposed to convince Nate not to resist, it had the opposite effect. Like a mad bull, he heaved up off the ground, wrenching his right arm free as he rose. He clubbed the man who had hold of him by the neck and the man's hold slackened but not enough for him to break loose. His other assailant was striving to clamp a hand on his wrist. Their combined weight caused Nate to trip and fall against the wall with a loud *thump*. He arced his knee up, and suddenly both his arms were free. Pivoting, he tossed one man over his hip.

Steel flashed in the starlight.

So much for them taking him alive, Nate thought.

The Wilderness series:

#47
WILDERNESS

REAP THE WHIRLWIND

David Thompson

LEISURE BOOKS   NEW YORK CITY

Dedicated to Judy, Joshua and Shane.

A LEISURE BOOK®

December 2005

Published by

Dorchester Publishing Co., Inc.
200 Madison Avenue
New York, NY 10016

ISBN 0-8439-5460-4

The name "Leisure Books" and the stylized "L" with design are trademarks of Dorchester Publishing Co., Inc.

Printed in the United States of America.

Visit us on the web at www.dorchesterpub.com.

REAP THE WHIRLWIND

Chapter One

The man who gave Nate King the idea did not know he had an idea to give.

Nate first spied the man across the lake. Nate was filling water skins for his family's journey when his bay snorted. He looked up and saw a line of riders emerging from the forest on the far shore. Instinctively, he reached for the Hawken that lay beside him. They were white men and not hostiles, but he still held the rifle level at his hip with his thumb on the hammer and his finger curled over the trigger.

There were five, the second to last with half a dozen big hounds on a long leash, the last leading packhorses. Their buckskins marked them as frontiersmen, their headwear as Southerners. Few from north of the Mason-Dixon were partial to coonskin caps.

Nate took several steps to the right so his horse

1

would not take a stray slug, should it come to that. Just because they were white did not mean they were friendly. As many savage men as savage beasts called the wilderness home, and it did not do to ever let one's guard lapse. His green eyes narrowed as the riders came close and reined up a dozen yards away.

"Good mornin' to you, sir," the foremost greeted Nate in a drawl as thick as molasses. He had a ruggedly handsome face with eyes the color of the lake. "Would these be the Rocky Mountains, or have I taken a wrong turn somewhere and ended up in South America?"

Nate's lips quirked in amusement. "South America, you say? No, welcome to darkest Africa, as folks call it. Keep on a spell and you'll come across a herd of elephants and some hippos."

The man laughed heartily, then gestured with the long rifle in his left hand. "As I live and breathe, a gentleman of refinement in the midst of this sea of fang and claw. My pleasure, sir. Robert Stuart is my handle, and these feckless individuals you see behind me are my kin. We left the great sovereign state of South Carolina five months ago and have been on the go ever since."

"That's a lot of traveling," Nate said. Walking over, he offered his hand and introduced himself.

"My goodness, aren't you the tall tree?" Robert Stuart said, shaking. "In my county I'm considered larger than average, but you would dwarf an ox."

Now it was Nate who laughed and said, "Is everyone in your county so excellent at exaggeration?"

"My God, a reader!" Robert Stuart declared.

"No one chucks out words of so many syllables without bein' as addicted as I am."

"I stand guilty," Nate said, and grew sad deep inside, for he had lost his precious collection of books not all that long ago and it would take him years to reacquire the volumes he most missed.

"I can always tell," Robert Stuart said. "Those who don't, like my brother Emory, here, use the puny words of a ten-year-old."

"Go to Hades," Emory Stuart said.

"See what I mean?" Robert winked at Nate. "Next he'll insult my ma, forgettin' she's his ma, too."

The other men, Emory included, were grinning, and Emory said, "We're mighty pleased to meet you, mister. We haven't come across another white man in a coon's age. Or maybe a possum's."

"They are scarce in these parts," Nate conceded. "But not scarce enough."

"How so?" Robert asked.

"How about if I tell you over a cup or four of coffee?" Nate proposed, and saw Stuart suddenly stiffen.

"What's this, then? You have a private army?"

Out of the trees at Nate's back had rushed four figures. One was a white-haired mountaineer with a beard halfway to his waist. Another was a swarthy youth whose features spoke of mixed lineage. With them was a girl all of sixteen summers and a warrior armed with an ash bow, an arrow already nocked to the sinew string.

"Is everything all right, Horatio?" asked he of the

white hair. "I was on my way down to the lake and saw them and went for help." He then indulged in his favorite pastime and quoted his namesake: " 'All furnished, all in arms, all plumed like estridges that with the wind baited like eagles having lately bathed.' "

"He called you Horatio?" Robert Stuart said. "I thought you told us your name is Nate?"

"Gentlemen," Nate addressed the Southerners, "permit me to introduce Shakespeare McNair. He has two distinctions. One, of having lived in these mountains longer than any white man alive. Two, of thinking he is a walking play and reciting the Bard nearly every time he opens his mouth."

Shakespeare put a hand to his chest in mock dismay. " 'From the extremist upward of thy head to the descent and dust below thy foot, a most toad-spotted traitor.' "

Robert Stuart said, "I do so adore a turn of the phrase, sir, and your phrases are turned most nicely."

"Credit old William S., not me," Shakespeare glibly responded.

The swarthy younger man was tapping a foot. "Enough of this silliness! Are they friendly or not?"

"My son, Zach," Nate said.

Robert Stuart leaned forward. "We can speak for ourselves. And yes, we are as friendly as the year is long to those who are friendly to us." His gaze shifted to the warrior. "Good Lord. They keep gettin' bigger. Does this one eat hills for his breakfast and supper?"

"Touch the Clouds is a leader of the Shoshones," Nate said, "and my relation by marriage."

Now the girl merited the South Carolinian's attention. "And who, pray tell, is this ravishing vision of female splendor?"

"My daughter, Evelyn."

"I have a girl your age back home," Robert Stuart said. "God willin', I'll be seein' her and the rest of my family before another couple of months go by."

"Amen to that," Emory Stuart interjected. "I miss my wife somethin' awful. Much to my surprise."

Shakespeare chuckled. "There's the rub. They drive us to distraction, but we can't toss them off cliffs."

"Uncle Shakespeare!" Evelyn exclaimed. "Wait until I tell Blue Water Woman."

"My wife is a Flathead," Shakespeare explained to the Stuart clan, "and she wields her tongue like a well-honed knife."

Zach had turned and was hurrying up the trail. Touch the Clouds lowered his bow and followed his example.

Dismounting, Robert Stuart handed the reins to Emory and came over to Nate. "Let me help you with those water skins."

"I'm obliged."

Shakespeare was going down the line of riders, pumping hands and repeating names. "Emory. Jethro. Arvil. Lee."

Evelyn had drifted toward the hounds. The big dogs sat still and silent, with their tongues lolling and their long ears hung low. "These are some critters."

5

"The best in Oconee County," Arvil said. He was lean and wiry and had a ready smile, and was not much older than she was. "They'll rip a bear or a cougar apart if we want them to."

Jethro nodded. "We breed them ourselves. Whenever there's a litter, folks come from miles around to buy one."

"They might tear a black bear apart, but never a grizzly," Evelyn said. She extended her hand toward the nearest hound, and it bared its fangs and rumbled deep in its barrel chest.

Robert Stuart turned partway and brandished his rifle at the dog. He did not take aim. He simply held it out in the dog's general direction. Instantly, the animal stopped growling and stopped baring its fangs and sat as meekly as a lamb.

"It's scared to death of you," Evelyn said.

"There's more to it than that, girl," Robert Stuart informed her. "A hound that won't heel or do what it's supposed to is as useless as teats on a boar. So we train our dogs right."

"I had a hound once," Shakespeare said. "One of the useless ones. He wouldn't hunt if I begged him. Whenever we saw a wild animal larger than a chipmunk, he ran the other way. I spent half my time catching him and the other half scolding him for being so craven."

"I wouldn't call it cowardly to run from a bear," Nate remarked. "I'd call it smart as smart can be."

"Says the gent who has killed more grizzlies than any man ever," Shakespeare teased. "You just wish you could run as fast as my hound did."

6

Robert Stuart asked, "Is it true about you killin' a heap of silvertips?"

"Unfortunately." Nate let out a sigh. "It's not as if I wanted it that way. I just seem to have a knack for running into them."

Shakespeare snorted. "There's no *seem* about it. You draw bears like a magnet draws bits of iron. The wonder is you weren't torn to shreds long ago."

"It's not for their lack of trying. I have the scars to prove it." Nate placed a hand to his side and a thick ridge of scar tissue from one of his more recent encounters. "If I had my druthers, I would as soon not kill another griz as long as I live."

The trail brought them to a clearing. In the center stood the cabin built by Nate's uncle, long since deceased, the cabin Nate had raised his son and daughter in. The home the King family had shared for going on two decades. Attached to the south side was a corral, which at the moment was empty. More than a dozen horses stood in front of the cabin, a travois attached to each animal. Some of the travois were heaped high with personal effects.

For the past hour, Nate and his family had been loading the few possessions they had left in the world. Not long ago, while they were off visiting civilization, their cabin had been ransacked.

"What's this?" Robert Stuart asked. "It looks like you're fixin' to move out."

"We are," Nate confirmed. "We're moving to a valley deeper in the mountains." To a haven no other white men had ever set eyes on, a sanctuary where he hoped his family would be safe from unfriendly tribes and the violent breed of whites who increasingly came to the Rockies. "Shakespeare and my son are moving there with us."

"What about this place?"

"It's stood empty before," Nate said. For months at a time on occasion. The wonder of it was that it had not been burned to the ground long ago by any of his many enemies.

"May I?" Robert Stuart said, and was almost to the threshold when out came two women.

Both wore beaded doeskin dresses. Both had long raven hair, the second woman's streaked with gray. Both would turn heads on any street in any town or city on the continent.

The younger woman stopped in surprise. "We have visitors, husband?" Her English was impeccable. "They have chosen an unfortunate time to come calling."

"They're only passing through," Nate said. To the Southerners he said, "This is the apple of my eye, my wife, Winona."

Robert Stuart doffed his coonskin cap and bowed with a flourish. "Maybe passin' through and maybe not, ma'am. It's a pleasure to meet you." Taking her hand, he kissed her knuckles.

"Oh my," Winona said.

"You must forgive my brother," Emory said to Nate. "He has long had delusions of bein' a grand gentleman. When he was little, he would practice bowin' and kissin' the hogs. We were the talk of the county."

"Pay him no mind, ma'am," Robert told Winona.

"He's an uncouth lout my mother has regretted not smotherin' in his swaddlin' clothes."

"They're both embarrassments," Lee Stuart said. He appeared to be the oldest and was also the quietest. "It's part of the reason we're thinkin' of pullin' up stakes and movin' to the Rockies."

"You're here scouting for a place to live?" Nate asked, but before any of them could answer, the last distaff member of his family, his son's wife, Louisa, came sprinting out of the trees as if her buckskin britches were on fire.

"Indians! Nine or ten of them, spying on us from the south ridge! I don't think they saw me, but I sure saw them!"

Nate was in motion before the words were out of her mouth. Swinging onto his bay, he called out, "Zach, Shakespeare, you're with me. The rest of you stay here." A slap of his heels brought the bay to a trot. He wound through the woods with a skill born of long experience, sticking to thick cover so the warriors on the ridge would be less apt to spot him. He slowed when the pines thinned, and soon came to a stop.

Shakespeare drew rein on his right, Zach on his left. Their rifles in hand, they were as grim as death.

"Want me to have a look-see, Pa?"

The brush crackled and Robert and Emory Stuart joined them. "I hope you don't mind us taggin' along," the former said, "but you folks have been so hospitable, it wouldn't be proper not to lend a hand if we can."

"Could it be more of your Shoshone friends?" Emory inquired.

"We're not expecting any," Nate said, "and there are too many tribes after my hair to take anything for granted." The Blackfoot Confederacy had long had him at the top of their list of whites they would most like to stake out and skin alive. The Sioux, too, bore him a grudge that stretched back years.

Zach raised his reins. "If you hear a shot, come on the run."

"There's a better way," Nate said. Twisting in his saddle, he opened one of the parfleches that served as his saddlebags, rummaged inside, and pulled out a folded brass telescope. He handed his Hawken to Zach, swung down, and stepped to a nearby pine. The prospect of getting sap all over his hands and clothes was not one he relished, but he started up the tree without hesitation, the spyglass tucked under his wide brown leather belt next to the flintlock pistols wedged on either side of the buckle. On his left hip was a Bowie, on his right a tomahawk. Across his chest were slanted his powder horn, ammo pouch, and possibles bag.

Nate climbed swiftly, careful not to rustle the limbs. He stayed on the side of the tree opposite the ridge, and when he was a good thirty feet up, he hooked his left arm around a branch, his body flush with the trunk, and pressed the small end of the telescope to his right eye.

The Indians were there, sure enough. Nine warriors armed with bows and knives. Their buckskins and the style in which they wore their hair marked them as Nez Percé.

Relief coursed through Nate. The Nez Percé were friendly. They lived many days' ride to the northwest and sometimes ventured to the plains after buffalo. It was a hunting party, not a war party. He thought he recognized one of the warriors from a rendezvous years ago. As he watched, they reined eastward to follow the ridge to where it would descend into the foothills and the prairie beyond.

Folding the spyglass, Nate descended and related what he had seen.

"All that worry for nothing," Zach grumbled.

"Better to worry and not have to kill than worry and be killed," Shakespeare said.

"I don't mind killing when it's called for."

" 'I wonder that thee, being, as thou sayest thou art, born under Saturn, goest about to apply a moral medicine to a mortifying mischief,' " Shakespeare quoted.

Zach cocked his head. "What in blazes did you just say?"

"Ignore him, son," Nate quickly said. "You know how he gets." He gave Shakespeare a stern look, and McNair laughed.

" 'I think the best grace of wit will shortly turn into silence, and discourse grow commendable in none only but parrots.' "

"There he goes again," Zach said, shaking his head.

Robert Stuart was beaming. "I could listen to

him all day. He's more entertainin' than a room full of kittens."

They started back, Nate in the lead and Robert alongside him.

The man from South Carolina cleared his throat. "About that cabin of yours. It would be a shame to neglect it. Ever thought of sellin'?"

"Not ever," Nate admitted. Even though he was moving, he was still fond of the place. Some of the best years of his life had been spent there. "Why? Are you planning to move to the Rockies?"

"It's the reason we came," Robert said. "To find a likely spot to homestead. This is marvelous country. All the tales we heard are true. Game everywhere. Peaks that rise to the sky. And the climate's not bad, neither."

"Wait until you've been here an entire winter, then say that," Nate responded. "Did those tales include mention of the dangers?"

"The hostiles and beasts and such?" Robert Stuart shrugged. "My brothers and cousins and me have every confidence we can protect our own."

"That's not confidence, it's delusion."

"How so? You've managed all these years, I take it? Your wife and offspring seem healthy and spry."

"We're alive only by the grace of Providence and a lot of luck," Nate said. "By rights we all should have died long ago."

"The good book says that God sends rain on the just and the unjust, so I reckon we have as much a share of that Providence as anyone else," Robert said. "And I've always been luckier than most."

12

"Luck won't keep the Utes at bay."

"How do they figure into this?"

"This is Ute territory. Other tribes pass through from time to time, but the Utes claim it as their own and they're not partial to outsiders. In the early days, they tried more times than I care to count to drive me and mine out. Later, I became friends with one of their leaders, and after I helped arrange a truce with the Shoshones and tracked down a grizzly that had been giving them fits, we struck a truce. But the truce won't apply to you and yours. The Utes will view you as intruders."

"I'll talk to them. I'll convince them to let us stay," Robert said with the utmost confidence.

"You're certainly welcome to try," Nate said, "but you would be better off picking another spot." He gestured at the vastness surrounding them. "It's not as if there isn't plenty to pick from."

"But I like this valley. That lake is right pretty. And those snow-crowned peaks would please my wife no end. She's always been fond of snow, but we get mighty little in Oconee County." Robert grinned. "Then there's a lot to be said for not havin' to break our backs buildin' our own place."

"It's not big enough for all of your families," Nate observed.

"But it would suffice until the others have built cabins of their own. So what do yuh say? Name your price. If it's not a king's ransom, I will fatten your poke."

"I'll consider it" was the best Nate could do. The notion was too new, too drastic.

"I can't ask more. As for the Utes, even if they won't see reason, they'll have the devil's own time drivin' us out with our hounds as our eyes and ears. We have over twenty more just like the ones you've seen, and they sic people as well as bears."

"They're well-trained."

"My great-grandpa was of the opinion that any animal can be trained if it's done right. All it takes is savvy and patience. Take Hector. You saw how he reacted when I wagged my rifle at him. He's seen what guns can do, and he doesn't want it to happen to him."

"You would shoot him?"

"Not ever, no. But he doesn't know that. What we do is catch game alive in snares and pits, rabbits and squirrels and deer and such, when the dogs are pups. Then we shoot what we catch and make the pups watch. They hear the blast and smell the blood, and after a while they catch on that a gun is death. From that moment on, they're in the palm of our hands."

"So you teach them to fear you."

"It's more than that. The whole idea to trainin' an animal is to change its nature to suit you."

"It wouldn't work with wild animals," Nate said.

"Who says? One of my uncles has a passel of tame raccoons. My pa taught a buck to eat out of his hand. My cousin has an owl that hunts mice in the field at night and roosts in his parlor durin' the day. Any critter can be trained if it's done right."

"There's no training buffalo or grizzlies."

"How do you know? Has anyone ever tried?"

14

"Most have too much sense," Nate said with a grin. "It's a lunatic's proposition."

"All I'm sayin' is that if it had to be done, it could be. Where there's a will, there's a way."

Nate chuckled at the silliness of it, but then he got to pondering, and by the time they arrived at the clearing he was seriously contemplating something only a lunatic would consider. The idea had fastened its teeth into him and would not let go. He was still thinking about it when the women put coffee on to boil.

Winona had invited their guests inside and was apologizing for not having furniture for them to sit on. "While we were east of the Mississippi a while ago, a bunch of renegades broke in and busted or smashed or ripped up nearly everything we owned."

"So you figure you'll be safer if you go farther into the mountains," Robert Stuart said.

"As safe as anyone can be in the wilds," Winona replied, "which is to say, not safe at all."

"The only thing that worries me about our new home," Evelyn mentioned, "is the huge grizzly that lives there. I've had my fill of bears, thank you very much."

"As have we all, daughter."

"I'll tend to that griz," Zach proposed. "After we're settled in, I'll track it down and have a nice new rug for my cabin. You would like that, wouldn't you, Lou?"

"Sure," Louisa answered.

"No," Nate said.

15

"No?" both Zach and Lou said at the same time.

"We're not going to kill it. I have a better idea. Or, rather, Robert here has given me one."

"What idea might that be, husband?" Winona wanted to know.

"I'm going to train the grizzly to leave us be."

Chapter Two

It galled Nate. Every time Shakespeare McNair looked at him, Shakespeare would grin or chuckle or stifle a laugh. For over an hour it went on. Then, as they were going from travois to travois to make sure everything was tied down, Nate straightened to find McNair chuckling at him yet again. "Enough is enough. I'm not that comical."

"Don't underestimate yourself," his mentor and best friend in all the world responded.

"What has you in stitches?"

"What else? 'You have not so much brains as ear wax,'" Shakespeare quoted. "I only hope you come to your senses before we get there, or we'll be planting you before the cold weather sets in."

"I can do it," Nate said earnestly.

"Will you listen to yourself? You might as well try to ride the sun or sleep in a rattlesnake den without being bit as to imagine you can ever tame a grizzly. It's preposterous."

"You only say that because no one has tried it."

"And no one has tried it because people in their right mind don't have a hankering to end their days as a pile of bear droppings." Shakespeare placed a weathered hand on Nate's shoulder. "Give up this fool notion before it gets you killed."

"I have to try."

"Give me one good reason," Shakespeare challenged him. "You can't, because there isn't any."

"I'm tired of killing bears."

"I don't blame you. You've had to kill more than most hundred men combined. That's hardly cause, though, to stick your head in the maw of a griz." Shakespeare studied him. "What's so special about this one that you'll take the risk?"

They were near the corral. Nate leaned back against the top rail, his elbows supporting him. "If I tell you, will you stop laughing?"

"I can try," Shakespeare said. "But you can no more change an animal's nature than you can turn a tree into a rock or a rock into a tree."

"You saw what the Stuarts have done with their hounds."

Shakespeare blinked and took a step back. "For God's sake, Horatio, they're *dogs*. Dogs and humans have been sharing fleas since before anyone can remember. Dogs train easy because we've been training them for so long."

"What will work for dogs will work for bears."

"You're pulling arguments out of thin air. Just

because bears have four legs and a nose and a tail doesn't mean they'll behave like dogs. No two creatures have the same nature. Bears are unpredictable and temperamental, and they have nasty teeth and claws, besides."

"Have you ever had a bear run from you instead of attack you?"

Shakespeare folded his arms across his chest. "I just said they were unpredictable, didn't I? Where one griz will charge, another might show its hind end. They're as individual as we are."

"So which is a grizzly's true nature? To attack or to run?"

"Oh. I see what you're getting at. Their natures aren't fixed in stone. And whatever isn't set in its ways can be taught to accept new ways. Is that basically the drift you're taking?"

"It's worth trying if it spares the griz."

"I repeat. What is so special about this one?"

Nate considered how best to explain. "The Indians call me Grizzly Killer. The Shoshones, the Flatheads, the Utes, the Nez Percé, even tribes that want to make worm bait of me, like the Blackfeet and the Piegans, they all know me by my Indian name of Grizzly Killer."

"And they call me Carcajou, or Wolverine, which is what the old-time voyageurs called me. Your son is called Stalking Coyote, your daughter is Blue Flower. How is that important? Names are names and nothing more."

"Not mine. Mine is more of a title. It was bestowed on me not because I resemble a grizzly or because a grizzly happened by as I was being born, as happened with Zach and the coyote. I'm called Grizzly Killer because when I first came to these mountains, hardly a month went by that I didn't kill one."

"Again, how is that important? Grizzlies were as thick as ticks back then. You're certainly not the only coon who tangled with them. I've killed over a dozen my own self. Hellfire, Blue Water Woman has had to kill two that were out to eat her."

"And lots of other mountaineers have killed them. Which is why there aren't near as many as there used to be. Grizzlies are going the way of the beaver and the mountain buffalo," Nate noted. The former had been virtually trapped out before the market for beaver plews dried up, and the latter had nearly been exterminated for food.

"I can't see it coming to that," Shakespeare said. "There will always be grizzlies. They're too tough and mean to be killed off."

"Not if everyone who comes to these mountains shoots every griz they see," Nate said.

"You're getting sentimental in your middle years."

Now it was Nate who took a step and placed a hand on the older man's shoulder. "I don't want to kill another bear. Not as long as I live. Not if I can help it. I've killed so many, I'm sick of the killing. Sick to my soul. Maybe it's stupid. Maybe it's wishful thinking. But I want this bear to be different. I want more than anything to live and let live this time."

McNair was quiet a bit. Then he smiled and clasped Nate's wrist. "I'll be of any help I can, Horatio. But there's one thing you should keep in mind, son."

"What's that?"

"This bear might not share your fine notion. It might see you as nothing but food. Or maybe it will go after Winona or Evelyn or any of the rest of us. What then? Do we turn the other cheek when one cheek has been ripped to shreds?"

"I'm not a dolt. If it comes to that, then yes, by all means, Zach gets his new bearskin rug."

"Whew!" Shakespeare exclaimed, and made a show of mopping his brow with a sleeve. "You had me worried. I was afraid your common sense had leaked from your brain."

"You should know better. I had too good a teacher." Nate squeezed the older man's shoulder.

Shakespeare glanced away and said thickly, "That damned sentimentality of yours is contagious. Let's check the rest of the travois so we can be on our way."

Nate had hoped to leave by ten in the morning, but it was past eleven when he offered his hand to Robert Stuart and said, "Again, you're welcome to stay for as long as you like. If and when you return with your kin, we'll discuss selling the cabin." He had not been able to make up his mind one way or the other.

Robert shook heartily. "Fair enough. It's been a pleasure makin' your acquaintance."

Winona, Evelyn, Zach, and Louisa were already

mounted. Shakespeare was giving Blue Water Woman a boost. Touch the Clouds was honing his knife with a whetstone.

Nate climbed on the bay and gigged it to the head of the line. A lead rope linked the horses pulling the travois, and he took hold of the end as he came abreast of the first animal. "A week from now we'll be at our new home," he announced.

Lou frowned. "It won't be a true home until our cabin is built."

Of all of them, Nate reflected, she had most resisted the move. She was attached to her old cabin, which she and Zach built with their own hands, and she had made no secret of her resentment. He understood, but it was best for everyone. Eventually, hopefully, she would realize that.

But Louisa was not the only one harboring regrets. "Good-bye, home," Evelyn sadly said to their cabin. "I'll miss you."

Shakespeare cupped a hand to an ear and tilted his head toward the log structure. "What's that? I didn't quite hear what you said?"

Evelyn chortled. "Cabins can't talk."

"They can't feel nor think, neither," Shakespeare said. "So why are you treating this one as if it can?"

"It's been my home for so long, I feel like it's part of me."

Shakespeare's grin dissolved. "Verily, I keep forgetting you are old beyond your years. After all that has happened to you, how could you not be?"

For one of the few times ever, Nate became genuinely mad at the man who had taught him all there was worth knowing about surviving in the wilderness. Just a few months ago, Evelyn had been through an ordeal that nearly cost her life, and Nate would prefer that Shakespeare not remind her of it. To distract Evelyn, he called out, "Here we go!" and started off.

"May God go with you!" Robert Stuart called out. "And thanks again for the use of your cabin!"

Nate did not look back. He did not trust himself. He felt as strongly about their homestead as Evelyn. Perhaps more so, since it had been his uncle's. He stared straight ahead until they crossed a ridge, so when he did finally glance back, the valley was not there anymore.

Hours went by. They were strung out over a hundred yards, Nate first and then Winona and Evelyn and Shakespeare and Blue Water Woman and Lou and Zach and Touch the Clouds. Countless times they had traveled together, but this time was different. The McNairs and Zach and Lou were giving up their homes to build new ones in the new valley, but it had not been their idea, it had been Nate's. They were making a sacrifice, a big sacrifice, to fulfill his wish of safety for all. Only time would reveal whether they had made the right decision.

The risks were enormous. For one thing, as the presence of the grizzly attested, the region in which the new valley was situated was rife with game, including all the different kinds of predators Nate had either driven out of the old valley or eliminated. The other risk was that there might be unfriendly tribes in the surrounding mountains, tribes that would prove to be as fiercely hostile as the Blackfeet or the Sioux.

But Nate was willing to gamble the move would prove worthwhile. The rewards were worth rolling the dice. Their new valley was a virtual paradise, much as the old valley had been nearly twenty years ago. Much as the entire front range of the Rockies had been before the trappers and the traders and settlers came.

It was a cycle, Nate thought. Like the changing of the seasons. A cycle that started on the east coast of the United States.

First to enter new regions were the frontiersmen, those hardy souls who lived off the land and who valued their freedom and their privacy more than the dubious benefits of civilization. But once they had been in a new region awhile, the wilderness was no longer wild. Hostiles were subdued, predators eradicated, and in flocked the settlers, the farmers, and others who rapidly took up all the remaining land and did more to depopulate the game than the few frontiersmen ever could.

Naturally, the frontiersmen moved on. They went in search of new land, new virgin territory where the conditions they enjoyed most prevailed, where there was land for the taking and game for the supper pot, and the cycle began all over again.

America's inexorable westward expansion, the newspapers called it. The manifest destiny to eventually claim all the land between the Atlantic and the Pacific. An entire continent of towns and cities and civilized society. The mere idea always depressed Nate. He hoped to God he never lived to see that day come to pass. He hoped to God there was never an end to the wilderness and the true freedom the wilderness afforded those willing to brave its perils.

Freedom came with a cost. The Revolution and the War of 1812 had proved that. It was a lesson Texicans learned not long ago, a lesson enshrined at the Alamo for all posterity. It was a lesson, Nate had noticed, taken for granted by far too many of his civilized brethren.

In his travels Nate had been to several cities. New York, where he grew up. St. Louis, the booming mistress of the westward tide. New Orleans, a bustling beehive of Old World and New. In all of them Nate had seen the same malaise—the widespread willingness to sacrifice freedom on the altar of convenience.

In the interest of law and order, citizens were willing to give up their right to bear arms. In the interest of having their lives run smoothly, they relinquished the right to run their lives to politicians.

Greed was rampant. Fine homes and fine carriages were what most craved more than anything. That, and money. Lots and lots of money. There were days when Nate was inclined to believe money had become the new Holy Grail. True, a person needed money to get by, but civilized folk were seldom content with a little. They wanted more and ever more, and to that end, they devoted their lives to its pursuit, the while neglecting the very freedoms that made that pursuit possible.

It was a strange world, Nate mused, made

stranger by humankind's insistence on reshaping the world in its image. Instead of learning to live in the wild on the wild's terms, most people wanted to bind all that was wild to their collective will.

One of Nate's favorite authors, James Fenimore Cooper, touched often on that theme in his fine novels. Nate missed those novels, missed all his books terribly. He had gone to Bent's Fort a couple of weeks ago and sent off for as many replacements as he could afford, but it would be months before they arrived. Until then he had to go without.

Robert Stuart was right. Nate had always been a reader. From his early childhood he had always enjoyed curling up with a book and letting his imagination run rampant. Books fed his mind as food fed his body. Books imparted truths and facts he could not find elsewhere. And books were the best entertainment around.

Lord, Nate loved books. So did Shakespeare, although McNair was content to limit most of his reading to the Bard. Nate once asked McNair why he was so fond of the playwright, and Shakespeare had replied, "He's salve for the soul. His words are like beacons of light in the dark irony of existence."

Suddenly, a sound intruded on Nate's contemplation. He heard it at the same instant that the bay nickered and shied. It was one of the most ominous sounds in all of nature, a harsh rattle such as that made by shaking a dry gourd with seeds inside, only this was no gourd.

The rattling came from a large rattlesnake coiled within striking distance of the bay's front legs.

Before Nate could bring his Hawken to bear, the bay reared. He had to clutch at his saddle to keep from being thrown. He saw the snake's head dart forward, its mouth wide to expose its venomous fangs. It missed, or he thought it did, and coiled to strike again.

The bay came down on all fours, its front hooves narrowly missing the rattler. Again the serpent struck, as swift as lightning, and this time, to Nate's horror, he was sure the fangs sank in.

Nate hauled on the reins to get the bay out of there, but the bay had a mind of its own. Again it reared, and again it brought its front hooves crashing down, the heavy thuds like twin sledge blows. One hoof missed, but the other smashed the rattler's tail. Uncoiling like a bullwhip, the snake thrashed wildly about. The bay reared yet again, and the rattlesnake instantly began to crawl off, but slowly, much too slowly.

The hooves caught it again, and this time both hooves came down squarely on the rattler's distinctive hexagonal markings. The snake's head came up off the ground and it struck madly about.

At last the bay allowed Nate to rein it aside, then stood with its nostrils flared and its whole body trembling.

The rattlesnake was on the move again, striving to reach cover, but moving sluggishly. Half its thick body had been crushed. Its skin was ruptured and its inner flesh was oozing out.

Snapping the Hawken to his shoulder, Nate fixed a bead on the serpent's triangular head. It was moving so slow that he was sure it would soon die anyway, but he thumbed back the Hawken's hammer and smoothly squeezed the trigger, coring the peanut brain and blowing half the snake's head off.

The bay was still quaking. Dreading the worst, Nate slipped from the saddle and knelt. He checked from the knee down to the hoof on the right leg, and then from the knee down to the hoof on the left leg, but could not find any puncture marks. Yet he had seen the snake strike. He checked above the knee on one leg and then the other. He checked lower down again, especially the area around the fetlock, and he still could not find the marks that had to be there.

"Anything, husband?"

Nate unfurled. Winona and Evelyn had ridden up, and the rest were hurrying to gather around. "Not that I can find." He knelt again, examining both hoofs closely. On the left one was a smear that might be venom. "We were lucky."

Zach arrived and vaulted from his zebra dun. Picking up the rattlesnake, he declared, "This will make a fine stew for supper." He drew his tomahawk, placed the snake back on the ground, and chopped off its head. Then, opening a parfleche on the zebra dun, he placed the mangled reptile inside.

By then Shakespeare and Blue Water Woman were there, and McNair made a sniffling sound and said, "Pity the poor serpent."

Nate had straightened and was about to climb on the bay. "How so?"

"It was just being true to its nature," Shakespeare said, "and you went and killed it."

"The bay did most of the killing. All I did was finish it off." The saddle creaked under Nate as he slipped his moccasins into the stirrups. "And you're not fooling anyone. You're trying to impress on me that just as a rattler must be true to its nature, a grizzly must be true to its."

"Will wonders never cease," Shakespeare said in mock amazement. "Is that a glimmer of intellect I detect? Or did Winona tell you to say that?"

"You have a deplorable sense of humor." Nate reined the bay westward.

"I like it," Winona said, "and I like his point even more."

She would, Nate thought. She was strongly against his idea of the bear, and had made her feelings clear in sharp tones before they left. Since they were busy getting ready to leave, he had postponed the inevitable clash by saying they should talk about it later. So far she had not brought it up again, but thanks to Shakespeare, she undoubtedly would, and soon. Women could be as tenacious as ravenous wolves. Nagging, whites called it. But Indian women, Winona had informed him many a time, never nagged. Strange, then, that it sure seemed like nagging to him.

The truth was, Indian women nagged as persistently as their white counterparts, in some instances subtly, in others with a viciousness that made one wonder if there was a darker basis for their nagging.

Nate would never say men did not deserve to be nagged. He was as prone as any man to not doing things the way his wife sometimes wanted them done. When a woman did not get her way, she might say it did not matter, and everything was all right, but it *always* mattered. Women were different from men in that regard, as they were in so many others. It often amused Nate, exactly how different they were. He once heard a trapper say that the Good Lord made a mistake in making women, but he disagreed. He could not conceive of life without Winona. She was everything to him— even if she did nag now and again.

More hours crawled by. Nate was absorbed in thought when a voice intruded.

"What are you thinking, husband?"

"About our new home," Nate said.

"About the bear, and about leaving me a widow?"

Here it comes, Nate told himself. "We're not even there yet and you have me buried? That shows a lot of confidence."

"Oh, I have complete confidence in the grizzly," Winona threw a pointed verbal dart. "Grizzlies kill people. It's that simple."

"Nothing in life is ever simple. And it's not as if I intend to walk up to it and talk it into leaving us alone."

"It's good to hear you have a shred of sense left." Winona did not yield a fraction. "More than any man living, you know how grizzlies are. You know they can never be trusted."

"Back east they tame black bears. True, they always keep the bears muzzled, because even the tame ones will bite. But the bears generally have mild dispositions."

"Is that supposed to make me feel better about your insane idea?"

"Have I ever mentioned how marvelous your English is? You speak it much better than I could ever speak Shoshone."

"Save your flattery, husband. I am immune. And I refuse to change the subject, which is the grizzly, and how you intend to go about persuading it to live in peace with creatures it views as prey. Namely, us."

"I haven't worked that out yet."

"Tell me. Is this because of the last bear attack you endured? The one that nearly killed you? The one you will carry scars from for the rest of your days?"

Nate grew warm about the neck and face. "That's the most insulting thing you've ever said to me. I'm no coward."

"Did I say you were and not hear myself say it? You are one of the bravest men I know. Too brave, at times, for your own good, and ours. This business of the grizzly puzzles me, is all. I am trying to understand."

"I'm sure you've talked to Shakespeare. Hasn't he explained?"

"He told me what you told him, yes, but he is as puzzled as I am. Your son thinks it is the silliest notion he has ever heard. Lou says this is the only stupid thing she has ever heard you say or do. Blue Water Woman has no idea what to make of it. And your daughter—"

"Your daughter hopes to God you know what you are doing." Evelyn had ridden up on the other side of him.

"So all of you are against it?" Nate asked.

"We care for you, Pa, and don't want you ripped to pieces," Evelyn said. "That's natural, isn't it?"

"I suppose," Nate admitted.

Hoofs drummed, and Shakespeare trotted close on his white mare. "My apologies for interrupting, Horatio. But Touch the Clouds thought there is something important you should know."

"I'm listening," Nate said, grateful for the reprieve.

"We're being followed."

Chapter Three

Nate's first thought was that the Stuarts were following them, although why that should be, he couldn't say. But when he brought the bay to a stop next to Touch the Clouds, the giant Shoshone pointed and said in the Shoshone tongue, "The Crow you like most of all Crows."

Nate groaned, and had to endure the giant's quiet mirth. "Go on ahead with the others."

"Do you want me to count coup on him?" Touch the Clouds asked, his shoulders moving up and down.

"Since when do warriors count coup on children?"

"He has seen sixteen winters. Or is it fifteen? I cannot remember." Touch the Clouds became serious for a moment. "He is not a child. Blue Flower is not a child. You do not see that because she is your daughter."

In English Nate muttered, "You sure are a big help."

Touch the Clouds said in Shoshone, "On the day she becomes his woman, I will give her three fine horses as a gift."

"Not if someone pushes you off a cliff first."

Grinning, Touch the Clouds trotted westward.

Nate sighed and placed his Hawken across his saddle. He did not need this. Not now. He harbored a secret hope that Touch the Clouds was mistaken and it was not who the Shoshone thought it was, but then a young warrior appeared off through the trees. "Hell," Nate said to the bay. "First the rattlesnake. Now him. It's not my day."

"Grizzly Killer!" The stripling waved his bow overhead. "It be me! Chases Rabbits!"

Nate tried to smile, but his heart was not in it.

"Something be matter? You look like sit on lance."

"Indigestion," Nate said.

"That be new word. What it mean?"

"It's what happens when you eat too much or drink too much or a tree falls on you." Nate did not add that some trees had two legs. "What on earth are you doing here?"

Chases Rabbits sat straighter and puffed out his less-than-impressive chest. He wore his hair Crow fashion, which was to say, hanging in loose braids on either side. Instead of a buckskin shirt he had on a beaded vest. His moccasins were also decorated with vivid beads of blue and brown. His leggings were fringed at the waist and around the ankles. Across his back was a quiver. "Me come visit."

"In your Sunday-go-to-meeting clothes?"

"Me be sorry. Not savvy." Chases Rabbits had learned English from a missionary, but he had not learned it well.

"It's nothing," Nate said. "We can't visit with you right now. We're on our way somewhere."

"Me know," Chases Rabbits said. "To valley, yes?"

Nate had to remind himself the young Crow had been with him when he found it. "To the valley, yes," he confirmed. "So it's best you go back to your village and visit us another time."

"Me want see Blue Flower. Think of her much since me see her last. Think she be good wife, good mother."

"I've told you before," Nate said irritably, "that my daughter is much too young to take a husband. She has no interest in marrying you or any other man."

"She will," Chases Rabbits said with the utmost confidence. "She learn like me. Come live lodge. We make many babies."

Nate inwardly counted to ten. "What will it take to get it through that thick skull of yours that she won't be ready to marry for years yet? She's just a girl."

"Me sister same winters. She have man. Me cousin younger. She have man. Me other cousin—"

Nate waved a hand, cutting him off before he recited every female about Evelyn's age in the Crow nation. "Your people tend to marry young, yes. But Crow ways are not white ways." He had made it as plain as plain could be, on several occasions, that under no circumstances would he consent to letting Chases Rabbits court Evelyn. But it was like talking to a tree stump.

"Me learn white ways. Me be good husband," Chases Rabbits said. "Help Grizzly Killer hunt. Help Grizzly Killer hunt deer. Help Grizzly Killer hunt elk. Help Grizzly Killer hunt buffalo. Help Grizzly Killer hunt—"

"That's enough. I get the idea."

Chases Rabbits was not done. "Me make Grizzly Killer much happy. Me make Blue Flower much happy."

The only thing that would make me truly happy, Nate thought, *is if you ride off and never come back.* Out loud he said, "Come to the valley in a couple of moons. We will talk more then."

"Me come valley now," Chases Rabbits beamed. "Help Grizzly Killer build new lodge of wood. Remember you tell about?"

Nate smothered another groan. On their initial visit to the valley, he had made the mistake of saying how much the new home meant to him, and how much work was involved in building a cabin and a corral. Let alone three cabins. "You really don't need to go to any bother."

"But we friends. Me like Grizzly Killer. Me like Grizzly Killer's daughter. Me like Grizzly Killer's

36

woman. Me like Grizzly Killer's son. Me like Grizzly—"

"I swear I'm going to shoot you."

"What? Why? Me show me be good"—Chases Rabbits stopped and his face scrunched up—"how you say, son-law?"

"Son-in-law."

"That be it, yes." Chases Rabbits nodded vigorously. "Son-in-law. Son-in-law." He rolled the words on his tongue like they were balls of hard molasses. "What mean in-law?"

"Related by marriage but not by blood," Nate elaborated, thinking the young Crow was putting the cart a mile ahead of the horse.

Chases Rabbits opened his mouth to say more but abruptly squared his slim shoulders and held his chin high in a posture of assumed manliness.

Nate did not need to see who was riding up behind him to know who it was. As she reined to a stop, he smiled thinly and said, "Look here, daughter. Your Prince Charming has come courting again."

"Hello, Chases Rabbits. This is a surprise."

"Good surprise, yes?" the young Crow said anxiously, his eyes aglow with the rapture of visually drinking her in. "Me ride many sleeps. Many, what you call them? Little word that mean long? Many miles! That be it! Have many dangers."

"Let me guess," Nate said dryly. "You were attacked by a horde of rabid chipmunks."

"Sorry?"

"Pay my father no mind," Evelyn said. "It's sweet of you to come so far to see me."

"Don't encourage him," Nate whispered.

"Sorry?" Chases Rabbits said.

"I told her you are a fount of courage," Nate said, and received a stern glance of disapproval from the fruit of his loins. He reined the bay around. "I need to join the others." Holding his hand so Chases Rabbits could not see it, he motioned sharply, saying in a low voice to Evelyn, "Get it over with, and catch up." Taking it for granted she would do as he wanted, he clucked to the bay.

In his more honest moments, Nate would admit to liking the young Crow. But the notion that Chases Rabbits and Evelyn would become man and wife was ridiculous. His daughter fancied herself to be a refined young lady and much preferred white ways to Indian ways. It was why she always wore a homespun dress. It was why she often expressed her heartfelt wish to move east of the Mississippi River in a few years and live in a town or city.

Nate was almost to the others when he looked back and was surprised to see Evelyn and Chases Rabbits riding side by side, talking and smiling. She had not shooed the young Crow off, as he advised. He figured she was being polite and would get around to it in a bit. Passing Touch the Clouds, he slowed to pace his son and his son's wife and brought up something he had been meaning to ask. "Harboring any regrets about the move?"

Zach shrugged. "One valley is as good as another to me so long as there is plenty of game."

"I'll miss our cabin," Louisa said. "It was our first home together."

"There's nothing to keep us from going back from time to time," Zach mentioned. "For as long as it's still standing."

"Oh, Zachary," Lou said.

"What did I do?" Zach glanced at Nate, who did not say anything. Long ago Nate had learned the painful lesson that some things in life, such as knowing when to keep one's mouth shut, came only with experience.

"I only meant it's likely the Blackfeet or someone else will burn it down," Zach justified himself.

"You'll love the new valley," Nate said to Lou to make up for his son's lapse in judgment. "I doubt any of our enemies know it exists. We should be perfectly safe."

"I wasn't born yesterday," Louisa said. "We're never safe out here. If it isn't a hostile out to count coup on us, it's an animal out to eat us."

Zach interjected, "That's why weapons were invented. Always keep a gun handy and you'll be fine."

"A good gun is a godsend, yes," Louisa said, "but guns do not solve all our problems."

"Did I say they did? But they can stop anyone or anything out to do us harm, and that's what's important."

"East of the Mississippi people don't need to go

around toting guns—or any other weapon, for that matter," Lou mentioned rather wistfully.

"Now you sound like my sister," Zach said testily. "As much as I care for her, her notion that the white world is better than the red world is as silly as silly can be."

"Evelyn has a point, though. I never once, the whole time I was growing up, worried about taking a lance in the back or having a bear rip my face off."

"You worry about those things now?" Zach asked, incredulous.

"What sort of question is that? Of course. Don't you?"

"Why fret about things in advance?"

Nate was inclined to ride on and be spared their dispute, but he wanted to hear more of what his son had to say. They thought so unlike, Zach and him, which was a source of great bafflement. He had assumed his son would take after him, but they were completely different in temperament and beliefs. His son was much more hotheaded and much more violent.

"You don't ever worry about a bear or a mountain lion catching you unawares or a war party catching you with your guard down?" Louisa was asking.

"I worry about that happening to you," Zach said.

Louisa's eyes flashed. "I'm inferior to you, is that it? I can't take care of myself? I need you to watch over me?"

"Once again you're putting words in my

mouth," Zach responded. "What is going on? Why are you taking my head off for no reason?"

"There are reasons and there are reasons."

"Oh, *that* made a lot of sense," Zach said. "You've been treating me like this since we came back from St. Louis after rescuing my sister from Athena Borke."

"You rescued her. I had no part in it," Louisa stated.

"You're mad because I saved Evelyn and you didn't? That makes even less sense. You should be happy I found her before something terrible happened."

Nate marveled that his son did not see why Lou was hurt when the truth was right there in front of him. He wondered if he had been as blockheaded when he was Zach's age. Maybe it just took a while for a man to learn to look beyond what a woman said to how she truly felt.

"I *am* happy you saved Evelyn, I'll have you know," Louisa said severely. "I am *not* so happy that you did it alone. That you took off without a word to the rest of us and left us to worry for weeks."

"So that's what this is about. But how can you hold it against me? I had to go when I did or we would have lost Evelyn for good."

"You could have sent word."

"I was always on the go. Always following leads. Always searching. There was no time."

"A poor excuse is no excuse," Louisa said. "Not

when all you had to do was scribble a few lines on a piece of paper."

"And get it to you how? Through the mail? As unreliable as it is? And to where would I have sent a letter? I didn't know where you and the McNairs had gotten to, remember?" Zach shook his head. "I did the best I could and I refuse to feel guilty. I'm sorry you are upset, but it couldn't be helped."

"You should have sent word somehow," Lou peevishly insisted.

Nate had listened to enough. He flicked his reins, saying, "I'd best get up ahead with Winona." They continued to argue as he rode off. He wound slowly through the timber, enjoying the sun on his back and the soft caress of the breeze on his face.

Nate did so love the mountains. He had loved them at first sight, as a man might love a woman at first sight. His first impression had been of a gigantic wall built by God, towering ramparts of stone and earth that rose so high into the sky, even in the summer the highest peaks were covered with snow. They were like nothing he had ever seen, the Rockies. So-called mountains back east could not begin to compare. They were hills. The Rockies were true mountains.

Nate had never realized it was possible to fall in love with a hunk of landscape. Oh, he had liked New York, liked his uncle's farm, so lush and fertile and rich with life. He had liked the parts of Pennsylvania he visited, and the coast of New Jersey. He had liked the desert country of the southwest. He had liked the perpetually wet forests of the northwest. He had seen both oceans and liked them. But he had not loved New York or Pennsylvania or the country around Santa Fe or the woodland along the Columbia River. The only place he loved, the only region that stirred him in the depths of his being, were the Rocky Mountains.

Sometimes Nate tried to work out in his head why he loved the Rockies so much. What was so special about them? The quality was hard to define. It was more than the size of the mountains. It had something to do with their character. Land, like people, had a character of its own, and the amazing thing was that no two people saw the character of the land the same way. One person might regard the desert as no more than baked sand and prickly cactus, while another might see it as the most beautiful real estate on the planet. One person might regard the bayou country of Louisiana as mosquito- and alligator-infested swamp, where another might fall in love with the varied tapestry of bayou life.

Or a person might regard the Rockies as no more than a big pile of dirt and rock, where another would see in them a living portrait of all that was magnificent and grand.

Nate never tired of their majesty. Of peaks that brushed the clouds. Of turbulent rivers and emerald lakes. Of vast forests of fir, pine, and spruce. Of mountain lilies and dogtooth violets. Of buttercups and yarrows and columbines. Of broad canyons and jagged ravines. Of monoliths sculpted by the wind and the rain. Of the feeling he had when he stood on a high mountain pass and gazed out over a vista of matchless splendor.

Nate would never leave. He would grow old and die there, and be buried in the soil that had nurtured him and his family in the guise of the game they ate and the vegetables they grew. He could think of nothing more fitting.

Nate considered himself luckier than most men. Luckier in the sense that he had found his niche in life. Most men went their entire existence without ever finding it. Without ever living where they most wanted to live and doing what they most wanted to do. It was rare for someone to be as supremely and truly happy as he was.

"A piece of pemmican for your thoughts, husband."

Nate looked up, annoyed at his lapses. There was a proper time for everything, and the proper time for deep thought was in the safety of one's cabin or lodge, or around a campfire late at night when all was tranquil. As much as he loved the wilderness, he must keep in mind it was a savage mistress with no sympathy for the unwary. "Louisa is still upset about Zach running off on us back east," he reported. "She hasn't forgiven him."

"Yes, she has," Winona disagreed. "She just hasn't forgotten. Women never forget. You should know that by now."

The female talent for recollecting the events of yesteryear had long impressed Nate. Winona, for instance, could recite every slight he inflicted from the day they became husband and wife. Half the time, he had to ponder long and hard to recall incidents she brought up. He had mentioned it to Shakespeare once, and remarked as how he thought Winona must be smarter than he was, but Shakespeare said no, that wasn't it, *all* women were the same.

"It's their nature. Women are the Almighty's way of keeping men humble."

"Read that in old William S., did you?" Nate had bantered.

"No. That's experience speaking. My first wife used her memory like a whip and beat me with it whenever she felt I needed to be put in my place."

"Does Blue Water Woman beat you, too?" Nate had grinned.

" 'You do unbend your noble strength to think so brainsickly of things,' " Shakespeare quoted. "Blue Water Woman is smarter than my first wife. She never whips when she can cajole. She never beats when she can entice. Her wiles and her memory work hand in hand, and combined they are unbeatable."

"Ah. Then I'm not the only husband to suffer daily defeats?"

"Are you jesting?" Shakespeare had rejoined. "A day doesn't go by that I don't suffer a dozen. My white flag long since fell into tatters."

Suddenly, Nate awoke to the fact that Winona was talking.

". . . noticed she has been snippy with him. But it will pass once she reassures herself that Zach loves her."

45

David Thompson

"How could she think different?" Nate asked. The depth of his son's affection for Louisa was as undeniable as it was perplexing. After all, Zach had always looked down his nose at whites because of the widespread white attitude that half-breeds were worthy only of contempt. His whole life long, Zach had to deal with bigotry. So for him to fall in love with a white woman had been a considerable shock.

"It's perfectly normal," Winona said. "There have been moments when I wondered if you really loved me."

Nate nearly drew rein in astonishment. "Haven't I made my love plain enough? Haven't I always done my best to make all your wishes come true? I gave you a roof over your head. You never wanted for food or clothes. You've always had a good horse to ride. What more proof could you need?"

"You don't understand," Winona said. "The proofs a woman looks for are not *things*. They are the little touches that come from the heart. How a man holds her, how he touches her, does he enjoy her company, does he talk to her, does he share all of him so their two hearts are entwined."

"I've always reckoned our hearts were one."

"Don't sulk. They are. The moments I wondered were early in our marriage when you would leave me for months on end to trap beaver. In the lonely hours of the night my heart would question my wisdom, but I was always there when you came back."

"I knew it was hard on you." It had been hard on Nate, too. He intensely disliked being sepa-

46

rated from her. She was as much a part of him as breathing.

Just then there was a holler from Shakespeare. He and Blue Water Woman had stopped and McNair had dismounted and was on bended knee, examining the ground.

"What has him so excited?" Winona wondered.

Large hoof marks were the reason. Not the distinctive oval tracks of unshod horses, with V-shaped gaps in the bottom, that would indicate the presence of a war party or a hunting party. These were the equally large tracks of buffalo, their cloven hoofs obvious. Often, on hard ground, the gap was not apparent, which was why greenhorns were prone to mistake buffalo tracks for horse tracks.

"Ten to twelve of the brutes," Shakespeare related. "I haven't seen a herd this size this high up in quite a while."

Nate nodded. Mountain buffalo were far fewer in number than their prairie counterparts. Fewer, shaggier, and with warier dispositions.

"None of us brought much fresh meat," McNair was saying. "What say we go hunting?"

"So soon?" Nate said. "We have a long way to go yet."

"The more meat we have now, the less hunting we have to do later. It would free us to spend more time building our cabins."

"He has a point, husband," Winona said. "You and I can go after a buffalo while the rest go on."

Shakespeare straightened. "I was sort of hoping

47

he and I could do the hunting. Like in the old days."

"And what about me?" Blue Water Woman asked. Years of living with McNair had made her as fluent in English as Winona.

"I'll think of your fair beauty every second and fly back to you when we have the meat."

"Flatterer," Blue Water Woman said.

Affecting a courtly bow, McNair quoted, " 'But, soft! What light through yonder window breaks? It is the east, and Juliet is the sun! Arise, fair sun, and kill the envious moon, who is already sick and pale with grief, that thou her maid art far more fair than she.' "

Blue Water Woman sighed and said to Winona, "Do you see what I must put up with?"

Shakespeare clasped a hand to his chest as if stricken. "She speaks, yet she says nothing. What of that?"

"Go hunt your buffalo," Blue Water Woman said.

" 'The brightness of her cheek would shame those stars, as daylight doth a lamp,' " Shakespeare quoted. " 'Her eyes in heaven would through the airy region stream so bright that birds would sing and think it were not night.' "

"I will stay, then," Winona said reluctantly. "But I do it for you, Blue Water Woman, and not for this reciter of scribbles."

McNair took a step back and sputtered, "Did my ears hear correctly? You *insulted* William S.?"

By then Zach and Louisa and Touch the Clouds had ridden up. Nate twisted in the saddle to scour the woods for his daughter and Chases Rabbits but did not see them. "Strange," he said aloud. "Where have Evelyn and that simpleton gotten to?"

As if in answer, at that instant a high-pitched shriek pierced the mountain air.

Chapter Four

Few cries strike pure terror into a parent as the scream of their child. Nate King was in motion before Evelyn's shriek died. Hauling sharply on the reins, he brought the bay to a gallop. He rose up off the saddle but could not spot her. A log appeared in his path, and the bay vaulted it with ease. He had to skirt a cluster of boulders, and then he was riding flat out and hollering Evelyn's name over and over.

Off among the shadowy woods to Nate's left something moved. He veered toward it and saw the silhouette of a horse. His daughter's horse, standing with its legs splayed and its ears pricked. His daughter was not on it. "Evelyn! Where are you?"

"Over here, Pa! Come quick! We need help!"

Crashing through a belt of short pines, Nate beheld every father's nightmare lent horrifying form and deadly substance.

Evelyn was on the ground, propped on her elbows as if in the act of rising when she froze, her gaze riveted on the tableau in front of her. As well it should be.

Also on the ground was Chases Rabbits, pinned by his horse. The animal was on its side, its eyes wide and empty, as dead as a horse could be thanks to a gaping wound in its belly. A horn had sheared into its side, ripping it open from its hind leg to its front leg, and many of its internal organs had oozed out, along with copious amounts of blood and other fluids. Its intestines resembled so much slick, coiled rope.

Beyond the stricken mount was the creature responsible. It possessed not one but two horns, wicked scimitars of destruction no animal, or human, could withstand, not even a grizzly. As black as pitch and curved to hook and rend, those horns were propelled by nearly two thousand pounds of sinew, bone, and gristle.

The creature was a mountain buffalo. Its brown coat resembled a shaggy rug, only a rug rippling with vitality and power. The beast blended into the shadows so well that a rider might blunder on it without realizing it was there. A massive body, short legs, and pronounced hump completed the brutish portrait.

As Nate drew rein, the buffalo's dark eyes, impossibly small for something so huge, swung from the fallen horse to the bay, and a huge front hoof pawed the soil.

Nate hoped to God the buffalo didn't charge. He might be able to outrun it, but then again, over short distances buffalo were as swift as horses, and sometimes swifter. His Hawken was in his left hand, but he did not use it. Buffalo were notoriously hard to kill, and if he wounded it, there was no telling the lengths to which its destructive impulses would drive it.

Chases Rabbits tugged on his pinned leg and muttered a few words under his breath.

Instantly, the buffalo switched its attention to the young Crow. Taking a ponderous step, it glared so intently as to shrivel Chases Rabbits where he lay.

"Don't move!" Evelyn urged. "Stay perfectly still and maybe it will go away!"

Sound advice, but Chases Rabbits reached over his shoulder to draw an arrow from his quiver. He turned to stone when the mountain buffalo took another step toward him and grunted.

"Evelyn!" Nate called out when she made as if to leap to the Crow's aid. "Take your own advice!"

The undergrowth crackled, and out of it swept Winona and Zach. After a single glance to appraise the situation, Winona spurred her mare between Evelyn and the buffalo, placing herself in danger to protect her offspring.

"Sis!" Zach bawled.

Nate opened his mouth to warn his oldest not to do anything rash, but he did not open it soon enough. For as always, Zach was quick to respond to a threat as he customarily did: with direct action.

Lashing his zebra dun, Zach gave voice to a war whoop, snapped his rifle to his shoulder, and fired into the buffalo's shaggy form from a range of only several yards. At the blast and the belch of smoke, the buffalo whirled toward him and lowered its massive head. In the blink of an eye, it attacked.

"Look out!" Nate yelled. Fortunately, the zebra dun did not slow, and in another moment it was swallowed by the vegetation. Snorting and bellowing, the buffalo plunged in after it.

"See to Evelyn!" Nate shouted at his wife, and raced after the behemoth. His son was a superb horseman, but a horse could not run as fast in woodland as it could on a plain. Mountain buffalo were under no such handicap. They lived in the forest and could thread through closely hemmed boles with unbelievable speed.

Ahead, Nate glimpsed a pair of hurtling shapes. The zebra dun was fairly flying, but it could not shake its remarkably agile pursuer. For all their bulk and their conspicuously short legs, buffalo were as nimble as mountain goats when they needed to be. They could change direction on the head of a pin, wheeling and turning like great shaggy dervishes.

Zach glanced back and did the last thing Nate would do were he in his son's moccasins: Zach grinned. Zach lived for times like this, for the pulsing thrill of a life-or-death struggle. Danger was a tonic to which he was addicted. Only experience would teach him the error of his passion, provided he lived long enough to learn from that experience.

Nate tried to fix a bead, but the buffalo was weaving and bobbing and he did not want to waste the slug. He must be sure when he squeezed the trigger. His son's life hung in the balance.

Then the brush parted and out of it sped a giant rider in buckskins, an arrow nocked to a sinew string. Touch the Clouds was guiding his horse by leg pressure alone. Sweeping in broadside to the buffalo, he unleashed two shafts in startlingly rapid succession.

For most buffalo that was enough. Nate had witnessed his friend bring down scores of the behemoths the same way. But either the arrows missed this buffalo's heart or this buffalo was possessed of extraordinary vitality, for instead of tumbling tuft over ears, the bull veered toward the giant Shoshone, its head dipping to do to Touch the Clouds's mount as it had done to Chases Rabbits's.

Just like that, Touch the Clouds shifted, and his superbly trained horse evaded harm.

No sooner did the buffalo resume its pursuit of Zach than Touch the Clouds angled in close once more and once again unleashed a feathered promise of death. But the buffalo denied the promise and, swinging its head in a vicious swipe, came within a whisker's width of disemboweling Touch the Clouds's horse.

Nate, meanwhile, was speedily coming up on the buffalo's other side. Preoccupied with Touch the Clouds, the buffalo did not realize he was there. Holding himself as steady as possible, Nate sought to take precise aim. It could not be done. The buffalo was moving and the bay was moving and he was moving with the bay's movements, and it would be a wonder if he put the slug anywhere near the great beating heart that drove the monster. Yet he had to try. So far luck had been with Zach, but no one's luck held forever.

Touch the Clouds had lost a little ground and was trying to make it up.

To their rear came Winona and, farther back, Shakespeare, neither within reliable rifle range.

His reins pinched between two fingers, Nate compensated for the rolling gate of the bay and fired. Much to his joy, the buffalo stumbled and almost fell. But almost did not count.

The shot had an unforeseen and unwanted effect in that the bull, in a burst of primal power, went faster than ever, and in a very few bounds its horns were nipping at the zebra dun's hoofs.

The death of his son was potentially heartbeats away. Drawing a pistol, Nate extended it and cocked the hammer. Desperate to forestall the inevitable, he did not aim, he simply fired at the buffalo's hairy side hoping to turn it. But fickle fate intervened, and a low tree limb struck his elbow just as he fired, jarring the pistol so that his shot went low instead of into the bull's ribs.

Even so, the buffalo stumbled and almost went down. It recovered quickly but slowed drastically, giving the zebra dun the opportunity to pull far enough ahead that Zach was temporarily out of peril.

Nate thought he had missed. Then he saw a scarlet stain on the right bull's foreleg. His wild shot had done what his well-placed shot and Touch the Clouds's arrows had failed to do.

The Shoshone had more of those shafts. Slowing

to match the bull's speed, Touch the Clouds sent three arrows into its hairy coat, one after the other. The *thunk-thunk-thunk* was punctuated by a rumbling snort.

Once more the bull stumbled. Pitching forward onto its front legs, the buffalo grunted and twisted its huge head, trying to see the bristling shafts that stuck from its heaving side like so many oversize porcupine quills. Blood trickled from both of its nostrils.

Looping around its horns, Nate drew rein beside his friend. The bull stared at them but did not attack.

Touch the Clouds regarded the buffalo solemnly. "We will have plenty of meat, Grizzly Killer."

"Do you want to do it or should I?" Nate asked.

"I will give it a quiet death," Touch the Clouds responded, notching another arrow to his bowstring.

Just then Zach hurtled out of the pines and reined his lathered mount to a halt. "Isn't it dead yet?" Springing down, he boldly and recklessly stepped to within a yard of the bull's head and took deliberate aim at a dark eye. "You nearly killed me, you son of a bitch," he said, and fired.

The eyeball exploded. The buffalo jerked to the impact, and a new sound, a sort of sustained groan, issued from its gigantic chest. Then its tongue lolled from its mouth and it slumped onto its side, its legs and tail twitching.

"You should not have done that, son," Nate said.

Misunderstanding, Zach glanced up. "Would you rather it suffer? When I kill something, I kill it. I don't let an animal linger in agony." So saying, he drew a flintlock, took a step nearer the still-twitching buffalo, placed the muzzle against its head, and cored its cranium.

The twitching and the groaning ceased.

"There." Zach shoved the pistol under his belt. "Now we can carve this critter up and be on our way."

Winona and Shakespeare had caught up and were watching without saying anything.

Dismounting, Touch the Clouds slung his bow across his broad back, then dipped two thick fingers in the red hole in the buffalo's head. Blood dripped from his fingertips when he pulled them out. He ran them across his forehead and across each cheek, leaving a bright smear.

"What is that for?" Zach asked.

"Respect," Touch the Clouds said.

"Meat is meat is meat." Zach turned from the slain animal. "Where's Lou?"

"She and Blue Water Woman are with the travois," Winona divulged. "Someone had to stay and keep watch."

"I'll fetch them," Shakespeare volunteered, but before he could rein about, Zach vaulted into the saddle.

"No, I'll go. Lou will be worried about me." Bestowing a grim smile of satisfaction on the buffalo, Zach rode off.

" 'A gentle riddance,' " Shakespeare softly quoted. " 'Draw the curtains. Go.' "

Only then did Nate's oversight hit him like a blow from a sledge. Stiffening, he exclaimed, "Evelyn!" and smacked his legs against the bay. He followed the path of crushed vegetation they had plowed through the undergrowth.

Winona galloped up next to him. She did not say anything. She did not have to. Her expression said it all. Nate had lived with her so long that he knew what was going through her head without being told; her thoughts were about their son, and her thoughts were his thoughts.

The chase had carried them farther than Nate realized. It took uncomfortably long to come within sight of the dead horse.

Chases Rabbits was still pinned beneath it. Evelyn was trying to lift the horse high enough for him to slide his leg out, but it was hopeless. Her relief was palpable.

"There you are! I was worried something had happened to you!"

Nate was off the bay before it came to a stop. He handed his Hawken to his daughter and sank to his knees. "Are you hurt?"

"Me legs have much pain," the young Crow said, "but me think me all right."

"Did the buff jump you?" Nate asked while sliding his hands under the horse as far as they would go.

"Buffalo charge. Me try get away, but buffalo too fast."

"It was me the bull was after, Pa," Evelyn revealed. "My horse reared and threw me, and Chases Rabbits rode between us."

"And lose horse," Chases Rabbits said sorrow-

58

fully, patting the animal's neck. "Best horse me ever have."

"You saved my daughter's life?" It challenged Nate's perception of the stripling as a bumbling half-wit. "We are in your debt."

Chases Rabbits motioned. "Do what need do. Save her for one day be my wife."

"Don't start that again," Nate said gruffly. Bunching his shoulders, he said, "Get set." He strained with all his might and puffed, "Try to pull your leg out! It's god-awful heavy."

"Me do." Chases Rabbits heaved backward, his palms flat on the ground for leverage. His leg moved a little, but not enough. "No can do, Grizzly Killer."

Nate relaxed. "We'll try again. This time, Winona and Evelyn will pull. Each of you grab hold of him under an arm."

When the two did so, Chases Rabbits giggled. "That tickle!"

"Concentrate," Nate said. He took several deep breaths, braced his legs, and lifted. He was a strong man. Some might say immensely strong. Yet lifting a horse was like lifting a mountain. He managed to raise the neck a bit higher than the last time, but although his wife and daughter pulled and pulled and Chases Rabbits pushed and pushed, the young Crow's leg stayed where it was.

"We might have to cut you out," Nate proposed.

"Cut horse?" Chases Rabbits was aghast. "Rather cut me."

"It's dead. It won't feel a thing."

"But me like horse. Be like cutting friend."

"Fair enough," Nate said. "We'll leave you here until you're hungry enough to eat your way out."

Chases Rabbits was suitably horrified. "It be like eating Grizzly Killer."

"Let's try something else," Winona suggested. "I will help lift. Evelyn, wrap your arms around Chases Rabbits's chest, and when we say so, pull."

As Evelyn obeyed, the young Crow's cheeks flushed. "Never have girl touch me there before."

"Don't make more of it than there is," Evelyn said. "As I keep trying to get it through that thick head of yours, we are friends, nothing more."

"Now we friends," Chases Rabbits said, "but moon from now, or moon after, maybe more."

"You're hopeless," Evelyn said.

"Me in love."

Nate sighed. "Me want to throw up." He firmed his hold. "Enough jabbering. Here we go."

"What be throw up?" Chases Rabbits asked.

Clenching his teeth, Nate bunched his shoulders. He could feel his muscles ripple and bulge, feel his whole body ache from the resistance. No man could lift a horse. But he had it to do, a tiny part of the horse, anyway, enough to free Chases Rabbits. It would not take much. Not much at all. His shoulders began throbbing and he could hear the blood roar in his veins, but the horse was solid granite, or felt like it was. Out of the corner of his eye, he saw Winona strain as he was straining, her face a beet.

Then Evelyn cried, "We almost have him!" Her

back was a taut bow and she was pulling for all she was worth. "The leg is coming loose!"

"Me come! Me come!" Chases Rabbits yipped excitedly, his own body arched, digging his hands into the soil for purchase.

Suddenly, like a cork popping from a wine bottle, the young Crow's leg popped out. Unable to brace herself, Evelyn fell on her backside with the Crow across her legs.

"Me came! Me came!" Chases Rabbits happily exclaimed, clapping his hands to his leg as if he could not believe it was still attached.

Nate slowly rose, wincing at a spasm in his lower back. His fingers were half numb and his arms leaden.

"I could not have lasted much longer," Winona panted, and grinned. "I will never again think my sewing basket is heavy."

Embracing her, Nate kissed her temple. "You did swell. Have I mentioned lately that you are the best wife any man could ever ask for?"

"Not in the last five minutes, no," Winona said. "So if you want to, go ahead. Women love endearments."

"Men call them greasing the axle," Nate teased.

"Do they, indeed?" Winona said in mock indignation. "It is the husband's fault if the grease runs dry. Endearments cost less than grease."

Chases Rabbits looked at Evelyn. "Me confused. What they talk about?"

"Wagons and such," Evelyn said, pushing him

off her so she could stand. Frowning, she brushed bits of grass and dirt from her dress. "Consarn it all. I'm a mess."

"You pretty," Chases Rabbits said. "Prettiest girl ever." He paused. "So sorry. Me must try harder to talk good. You prettiest girl there ever be. How that?"

"You're an adorable liar."

Furrows lined the Crow's brow. "What mean adorable?"

"Cute, like a bunny rabbit," Evelyn informed him.

Chases Rabbits's indignation was not feigned. "Me man! Me warrior! Me not bunny!"

"You chase them, don't you?" Laughing, Evelyn patted his head. "How else did you get your name?"

"Me get it when little. When boy of seven winters. One day see rabbit, try catch for to eat. Uncle see, call me Chases Rabbits. So all call me same." The Crow scowled. "Me not like name, Blue Flower. Not like any bit."

"You can pick a new name, can't you?" Evelyn inquired. "A Shoshone can change his."

"Can have new name, yes. But not pick. Must"—Chases Rabbits scrunched up his face, intent on the right word—"must make new name. Savvy? Make name? Live name?"

"Yes, I understand. You must earn the name." Evelyn smoothed her sleeves. "I hope you earn a name you like."

"Thank you. Blue Flower much sweet."

Nate had been scanning the forest. "Which way did your horse run off?" he asked his daughter.

"East. It must be halfway home by now."

"I'll go after it," Nate told Winona. "Take these two to the buffalo. Chases Rabbits can help Touch the Clouds and Shakespeare carve it up while you ride double with Evelyn and bring the packhorses."

"You better hurry, husband," Winona said.

Nate nodded. She knew as well as he did that if he was to have any hope of overtaking Evelyn's panicked mount before it reached the cabin, he must head out right away. Forking leather, he was about to jab his heels against the bay when Evelyn thrust the Hawken at him.

"Don't forget this. You're in the wilds, remember? Or don't you want to live to a ripe old age, Pa?"

"You have a tart tongue, daughter," Nate tenderly chided.

The bay was tired from chasing the buffalo, but it came to a trot in response to Nate's goading, and he held it to the trot for over half a mile. He had hoped that Evelyn's horse had not gone all that far, that its panic had soon faded and it had stopped to graze, but he passed several clearings and a small meadow and there was no sign of it.

"Fright is your kind's one weakness," Nate said to the bay. Fear was the one emotion horses could not control. Were it not for that quirk in their dispositions, they would be as dependable as those hounds of the Stuarts.

His bay was braver than most. But it, too, was prone to panic on occasion, invariably when his life was in jeopardy.

After a while, Nate realized Evelyn's comment was more true than she imagined. Her mount would not stop until it reached their cabin and the corral that had been its home since it was a colt. Nate wouldn't get there until late in the day, and since the bay and her horse would need to rest overnight, he wouldn't be able to start back to his family until morning.

Nate did not like being away from them that long. Now that he no longer trapped for a living, he did not enjoy being separated from Winona for even one night. He was tempted to forget the stupid horse and turn around, but Evelyn would be upset. She had ridden that animal since it was big enough to saddle. She was used to it and would not want to ride another.

So Nate kept going. But he was not happy. First the incident with the rattlesnake, then the incident with the mountain buffalo, and now this. It was one thing after another. Bad omens, a superstitious person might say. Thank God he wasn't superstitious and never had been. When he was a boy, he would walk under ladders on a dare, and let his neighbor's black cat cross his path to prove it had no effect.

Once Nate deliberately broke his father's mirror, but that was more because he was mad at his father for hitting his mother than it was to test the superstition of seven years' bad luck.

Hours passed, and the bay came to the last rise before the valley. Nate drew rein and fondly regarded the lake in the distance. A twinge of regret filled him. As much sense as it made to find a new place to live, he would miss his uncle's cabin, miss it a lot. A rush of fond memories flooded through him, and he smiled at the recollections.

Nate could not see the cabin. He was about to go on when an abrupt flurry of sounds came from the cabin's vicinity, sounds that were a bad omen in themselves: a chorus of whoops and the crackle of gunfire.

Chapter Five

There were ten of them. Ten that Nate counted through his spyglass; there might be more, but if so they were well hidden. The ten were dispersed around the cabin, three to a side except to the east, where there were four. They were not hostiles, as Nate expected. Not hostile Indians, anyway. They were white. Their clothes stamped some as river rats, others as the sort of city toughs Nate had seen many times. They looked out of place in the wilderness.

It was easy to spot their leader. He was different from the rest. Tall and lean, he wore a store-bought hunting outfit, as it was called. Buckskins dyed green, with knee-high moccasins and a green cap. Similar outfits were enormously popular in the States, but no true frontiersman of Nate's acquaintance would wear them.

For one thing, the shade of green was not the green of grass or the green of pine trees, but a strange shade that always reminded Nate of baby vomit. Once, when Zach was an infant, Winona fed him some mashed wild peas, which Zach did not take to. Green buckskins always reminded Nate of what came up.

For another thing, store-bought clothes were held in generally lower regard than home-sewn garb. Store-bought buckskin was of low quality, and the stitching was invariably shoddy.

But the tall man in green certainly looked impressive. He had an angular face with a hawkish nose and a chin that jutted in a point. A brace of pistols adorned his waist, as did a long knife sheath.

Nate had never set eyes on the tall man or any of the others. Why, then, had they attacked the Stuarts? Two horses that belonged to the Stuarts lay dead near the cabin door. Of their other mounts there was no trace.

Folding the spyglass, Nate descended the pine he had climbed. He must find out what was going on. The bay was in a thicket a hundred yards back, and he would leave it there.

No more shots boomed out as Nate crept along. Evidently, the cabin was under siege. How long the Stuarts could hold out depended on how much food and water they had with them.

Presently, Nate went to ground. Holding the Hawken in front of him, he crawled to where he had an unobstructed view of the front of the cabin, and of the four men in the woods facing it. The window had been shot out. It angered him greatly. That pane of glass had cost a pretty penny, and had not been easy to come by.

Nate had a clear shot at the tall man in green, but he did not take it. He would not shoot anyone until he had a better understanding of what was going on. Barely had the thought crossed his mind when the man in green cupped a hand to his thin lips.

"Can you hear me in there, King?"

"How many times must I tell you!" came Robert Stuart's reply. "Nate King isn't here!"

"I wasn't born yesterday," the man in green shouted. "You and your friends throw out your guns and step out with your hands in the air and we'll get this over with. What do you say?"

"Go suck on a sow!"

"Be sensible! We have you surrounded. We can sit out here until Armageddon if need be. But it won't take that long to starve you and your family out."

"What family would that be?" Robert Stuart responded. "Did you see any women or sprouts when you snuck up on us? There's just me and my two brothers and my two cousins. Our last name is Stuart, not King."

As Nate recollected, Emory and Arvil were the brothers, Jethro and Lee were the cousins.

The tall man in the green outfit laughed. "You'd like me to believe that, wouldn't you? But I was given a map with precise directions on how to find this cabin. Nate King's cabin."

"But King isn't here!" Robert roared. "You've made a mistake, whoever in hell you are!"

"Traggard is my handle," the tall man shouted.

"Lucian Traggard. Perhaps you have heard of me. In the bayou country my name is well known."

"Don't flatter yourself," Robert Stuart yelled. "To me your name might as well be Jackass."

At a harsh command from Traggard, a volley rang out. But the cabin walls were as thick as a fort's, and proof against most bullets. Nate doubted a single slug penetrated.

A laugh from Robert Stuart confirmed it. "Keep wastin' your lead! It's less you'll have when we bust out!"

"Please try!" Traggard baited him. "I need your head in my hands."

"My head?"

"I need it to collect the bounty," Lucian Traggard shouted. "We don't get paid if we don't offer proof you're dead. So I figured I'd take back your head, King."

"You're an idiot brought into this world by simpletons" was Robert's retort. "You have the right cabin but the wrong people! And so help me God, before this is over we'll teach you the error of your idiot ways."

"I'm trembling in my moccasins," Traggard taunted. "We have you at our mercy, and you damn well know it." He crooked a finger at a short unkempt associate with a tangled mess of a beard and filthy clothes. Whispers were exchanged, and the filthy one darted to the trail to the lake and hastened down it.

Nate shadowed him. He knew the area around the cabin as he knew the hairs on his chin: every tree, every bush, every boulder. Invisible to casual scrutiny, he paralleled the trail and discovered two more raiders with twelve saddle horses and six packhorses on the lakeshore. The filthy man made straight for them.

"The boss wants one of the kegs."

"What does he need that much for, Jigger?" asked a chunk of muscle with a neck as thick as the bull buffalo's.

"He didn't say, Huff, but he wants it right quick, and I wouldn't keep him waiting, the mood he's in."

Huff and the other man stepped to a packhorse and began undoing one of the packs. "I'll be glad when this is over. I miss New Orleans."

"I don't," Jigger said. "What's there besides grog shops and whores? I like these mountains, like them a lot."

"You can have them and the hostiles that live in them and the beasties besides. The Rockies might look like the Garden of Eden, but from what I've seen and heard, they're a garden of terror."

"Why, Huff," Jigger said mockingly, "since when did you become timid? You were raised in the backwoods, for God's sake."

"The woods of Ohio are a far cry from these mountains. There's not a settlement within five hundred miles, unless you count Bent's Fort, and that's a trading post."

"So?" Jigger said. "I've never been all that partial to people. I wouldn't mind living alone the rest of my days."

Huff and the other man were lowering something

bundled in a blanket. Unraveling it, Huff tapped a keg of gunpowder. "Here it is. What else?"

"This will do." Jigger stooped and wrapped his left arm around the keg. "Hold tight to the horses. In a short while there will be a powerful loud noise."

"Traggard's not doing what I think he's doing?" Huff said. "Why not wait the poor bastards out?"

"Do you think he hasn't thought of that? But they could have enough victuals to last a week, and Lucian wants it over with."

"I don't blame him," Huff said. "I have big plans for my share. There's a certain gal back in Ohio who said she'd always wait for me, and I aim to hold her to her word."

"Spare me your romance." Jigger moved toward the trail. "To me women are as worthless as a bucket of spit." He glanced back. "Remember. Hold on to the horses. We don't want to spook them and be stranded afoot."

"We'll watch them," Huff promised.

Jigger passed within eight feet of Nate but did not see him. Nate let the small bundle of filthiness go. Inching near to the edge of the trees, he watched as Huff and the other man gathered reins and lead ropes.

"When do you reckon it will be?" asked the second man, with a look in the general direction of the cabin.

"A while yet," Huff said. "They have to plant it close enough to do the job right. Relax, Veckers. Traggard knows what he's doing."

Veckers was a nervous beanpole. He gnawed on his lower lip as if it were chewing tobacco. "I hope so. Frankly, I regret letting him talk me into this lunacy. It all seemed so grand and exciting back in New Orleans. I mean, I had never set eyes on the frontier. I thought it would be a wonderful adventure."

"Instead it's hardship after hardship," Huff said.

"Exactly. We nearly starved several times on the way out. And that bear that killed Kostlan! I never thought there could be such a monster!"

"There are more grizzlies where that one came from," Huff said, bobbing his stubbly chin at the encircling peaks. "These mountains are crawling with them."

Veckers's Adam's apple bobbed. "I'd rather not be reminded, if you don't mind. They scare me like nothing else ever has. Look at how many shots it took to kill the one that ripped Kostlan apart. Eighteen. I counted them."

"That's why Traggard hired on so many of us. There's safety in numbers."

"There still aren't enough of us," Veckers said. "An entire army wouldn't be enough."

"Stifle yourself," Huff said in mild disgust. "You're starting to sound like a weak sister." He turned toward the lake. "Look at all those ducks. After we're done with the cabin, we should shoot some for supper."

Veckers turned, too. "It is pretty country. I'll give the Rockies that."

"They're tickled to hear it," Huff said, and inhaled deep of the mountain air. "Me, I like these Rockies. Like them a lot. I have half a notion to come back here someday and set down roots."

"What about all the hostiles?"

"There you go again. If fretting were gold, you'd be richer than John Jacob Astor ever was."

Nate rose and moved into the open, the Hawken level at his waist. Avoiding a few windblown twigs, he stalked close enough to see the short hairs at the nape of their necks. He thumbed back the Hawken's hammer.

At the metallic click, Huff went as rigid as a plank. Veckers, however, was true to his high-strung nature and whirled, stabbing for a flintlock at his waist.

"I wouldn't," Nate warned, shifting the muzzle so it was squarely on Veckers's chest. "You'll be dead before you clear your belt."

Veckers jerked his hand off his pistol as if it were a red-hot coal. "Who are you? What do you want?"

"I'm Nate King. I want the two of you to drop your guns and your knives and hold your arms out from your sides."

"*You're* King?" Veckers bleated. "But you're supposed to be trapped in the cabin with the rest of your family!"

"As the man inside keeps telling your boss, my family isn't at home," Nate said coldly. "Now, shed those guns."

Veckers glanced anxiously at Huff, who had not moved nor looked around. "What do we do?"

"What else?" Huff slowly rotated, wisely holding

his arms away from his body, and when he was all the way around, he let go of the reins he was holding and ever so carefully dropped his two pistols to the earth. The whole while, he intently studied Nate. "So you're the one with the bounty on his head."

"You must have me confused with someone else. I'm not wanted by the law." Nate still had the Hawken trained on Veckers, who had yet to disarm.

"Who said anything about the law?" Huff responded. "The bounty was posted by a private party on you and yours."

"What's that?" Nate was stunned.

"You heard me. There's a ten-thousand-dollar bounty on your head, and that of your woman and your brats. To collect it, all four of you have to be killed."

"Maybe you shouldn't be saying so much," Veckers said.

"Why not? What good will it do him?"

Nate was trying to emotionally absorb the revelation. *It couldn't be!* was his natural reaction. Yet plainly, the man was telling the truth. "Who posted this bounty?"

"You'll have to ask Lucian Traggard," Huff replied. "We're not privy to the particulars."

Ten thousand dollars, Nate thought. Good God, that was a lot of money! It spawned a host of questions evidently only Traggard could answer. But first things first. "Your guns," he said to Veckers.

The beanpole licked his lips.

"Don't be stupid," Nate said. He did not like

74

standing there with his back to the trail. Someone might come down it at any moment. Then there was that keg of powder. He needed to deal with these two and get to the cabin.

"All right, all right," Veckers said sullenly. He slid both pistols from under his belt and tossed them down beside Huff's. "There? Satisfied?"

"Not yet." Nate had to render them harmless. Common sense dictated he shoot them, but the shots would be heard. He had his Bowie and tomahawk, but they would resist and likely shout for help. "Walk to the lake."

"Why?" Veckers asked suspiciously.

"For a better look at the ducks." Nate wagged the Hawken. They both obeyed, but they were not happy about it, and Veckers had the aspect of a small animal girding itself to bolt. "You won't get five feet," Nate said to forestall the attempt.

There was no wind. The water was calm, the surface a placid mirror, undisturbed save for ripples created by the scores of various waterfowl.

"What now?" Huff wanted to know.

"Now you go for a swim."

"Like hell," Veckers said. "If I do, I drown."

"If you don't, you die."

Veckers glared at Nate. "You don't understand, mister. I can't swim worth a lick. I never learned."

"Then you're overdue." Suddenly moving forward, Nate jabbed him in the spine with the Hawken's muzzle. "In you go."

Huff had barely hesitated. He was in up to his knees, placing each foot with care. Of the two of them, he was the smarter; he knew Nate would not kill them so long as they did as Nate told them. The water rose to his waist and then to his chest. "How far out do you want us to go?"

"The middle of the lake would be nice."

Veckers had inched into the water but now stopped. "I can't swim that far! Listen to me!"

"Your friend will help you."

"Like hell." From Huff. "Likely as not, he would pull me under. He's on his own in this."

"Damn you!" Veckers snarled. "I thought we were friends? How can you say a thing like that?"

"Friends, hell," Huff said. "I put up with you. I listen to your gripes. I listen to you moan and complain. But we were never friends and never will be."

"Hell." Veckers clenched his fists. "Hell and hell again. You think you know someone. You think you can trust someone."

"Trust your whore of a mother, not me," Huff said. He was in the lake up to his neck. Another couple of steps and he must swim.

"Too slow," Nate said to Veckers. "Stop stalling."

"Do you have eyes? Can't you see I'm scared? I tell you I can't swim, but you ignore me. I'll drown, damn it!"

"Or be shot," Nate bluffed. "Take your pick." He was thinking of that keg of gunpowder.

Veckers managed several small steps, saying, "You were never anything to me, King, until now. Just a name. Just a lot of money once you and your family were dead. But now I hate you. Now I want you dead for me."

"Only a fool would come all this way to murder someone he didn't know," Nate remarked.

"Yes, I'm a fool," Veckers agreed, "for letting Traggard talk me into this madness. Easy money, hell! I should have told him no the moment he mentioned the Rocky Mountains."

"You talk too much," Nate said. "Start swimming."

"I talk when I'm scared. I can't help it. And as I keep reminding you, I *can't* swim!" Veckers spewed a string of obscenities.

Huff said, "Watch that mouth of yours. You'll make him mad."

"Do I care?" Veckers snapped. "Let him shoot me! It will be quicker than drowning."

Nate was still thinking of that keg of powder. He shifted his weight from one foot to the other and lightly rubbed his forefinger up and down the trigger. Very lightly, so it would not go off.

Huff was swimming as a dog would swim, paddling with his neck and head well above the water, making for the middle of the lake, as he had been told.

Veckers had yet to take a stroke. He was in up to his chest and moving more slowly than ever, his spindly arms wrapped to his bony sides and his whole skinny body shaking from fear more than the cold water. "I hate you, Nate King. Whoever wants you dead has the right idea."

"You don't know who is paying the bounty?"

"Only Traggard knows, and he won't say. Probably so none of us can claim the money, after. How he found out about it, I couldn't guess." The water had risen to Veckers's neck, and he stopped. "I can't do it. I can't go another step."

"The choice isn't yours to make."

"Shoot me, then, and be done with it." Veckers faced around. "This is as far as I go, so help me God."

Nate glanced toward the trail and the cabin. He tried one more bluff. He pressed the rifle's stock to his shoulder and sighted down the barrel. "Then I will blow your head clean off."

"Get on with it!" Veckers said bitterly. "I'm freezing and I soiled myself, and if I go any farther, I'm a goner."

It was just Nate's luck to have to contend with a coward. The other one, Huff, was forty feet out and paddling briskly. Lowering his rifle, Nate left them for the moment and stepped to the horses. He picked up a rock and threw it at one, and the horse shied but did not run off. He threw another and then a third, and kept throwing until some of the horses were prancing and whinnying in agitation.

The next rock Nate threw struck the flank of a buttermilk, and the buttermilk nickered and trotted to the south. Two packhorses followed it. Then four saddle horses. Then they were all in motion, their hoofs drumming, but not quite loudly enough, Nate hoped, to be heard by the would-be bounty

78

killers at the cabin. He threw a last rock to speed the animals along.

The keg of powder had its claws in his mind and Nate could not shake it off. He spun to run up the trail, and because of the drumming hoofs he did not hear the squishy patter of rushing feet until his attacker was almost upon him.

Nate whirled back around. The knife Veckers swept at his chest struck the Hawken, instead, and was deflected. He backpedaled to gain room to move and Veckers came after him, pressing him, swinging and thrusting and stabbing. Veckers's features were contorted in bloodlust. The man yearned only to kill.

Nate blocked another blow, sidestepped a thrust, evaded a stab. He slid both hands to the Hawken's barrel, and when Veckers lanced the knife at his groin, he swung the Hawken like a club.

The heavy stock caught Veckers on the side of the head. That should have done it. That should have rendered him insensate. But Veckers, for all his cowardliness, was stronger than he looked. Although his knees buckled, Veckers did not crumble. Steadying himself, he came in fast and furious, stabbing and slicing, slicing and stabbing. But his were city reflexes. The reflexes of someone born and bred to an easy life. Nate's were wilderness reflexes, finely honed by years spent in the wild on the razor's edge of existence.

The soft reflexes of a pampered existence against the lightning reflexes of a mountain panther.

It was no contest.

Veckers thrust yet again, his eyes on the Hawken, always on the Hawken, since it was the rifle that had hurt him. It was the rifle Nate kept using to block his blows. He had his eyes on the rifle, and he stabbed at Nate's throat and he never saw Nate's hand swoop to the tomahawk at Nate's hip. He did not notice the blur of Nate's wrist. But he felt the tomahawk bite into his neck, felt the sharp sting and then the sharper pain and the wetness of spurting blood, and Veckers lurched to a halt and clasped a hand to the wound to staunch that which could not be staunched this side of the grave. "No!" he cried. It came out as a bubbly gurgle, because there was blood in his throat and blood was gushing from his mouth and both nostrils.

"Yes," Nate said, and swung again, at a point above the ear. The blow jarred his arm, but the deed was done.

Veckers melted, his body quaking more violently than it ever had in the lake. He was caked scarlet from his chin to his waist. The knife slid from fingers gone limp. His eyes fixed on the sky and locked there. One instant they mirrored life, the next instant they dulled to emptiness.

Nate had delayed far too long. He spun and started for the trail, then heard splashing. Spinning, he saw Huff emerge from the lake and barrel toward the guns Nate had made them drop.

Huff had tried to trick him. Huff had turned back to shore the moment his back was turned, and thanks to Veckers, in three or four more strides he would have a pistol in his hand.

Nate gauged the distance and threw. Not a rock, as he had at the horses. He threw his tomahawk as he had practiced throwing it countless times before. The trick was to hold it near the bottom of the handle and throw it forcefully but not too forcefully, and to avoid snapping the wrist. A smooth throw was the key, and when done right, the tomahawk would do as this tomahawk did and perform a complete spin in the air and embed itself in the target, which was Huff's chest.

Huff reacted as if he had slammed into a wall. He stopped short and gaped at the steel stuck deep, then grasped the handle and pulled with all his might. The tomahawk came loose. But pulling it out was a mistake. The pressure of the blade had held most of the blood back. Now a crimson fountain sprayed. Within seconds, Huff had lost so much blood he was too weak to stand. He pitched to his knees, gave Nate a bewildered look, then folded, coming to rest with his forehead on the ground and his arms spread as if he were hugging the earth.

Swiftly reclaiming the tomahawk, Nate wiped it clean on Huff's clothes, slid the handle under his belt, and sped toward the trail, spurred by the persistent image in his mind of the keg of powder and what it could do to his cabin and those inside.

Chapter Six

Lucian Traggard and two of his mercenary companions were huddled by the south wall of the cabin. They had slid through the corral rails and crept to the lean-to in which Nate stored logs for the winter, and from there snuck to the wall. Crouched at its base, Traggard held the keg of powder while Jigger and another man dug a hole using their knives and their fingers.

Nate was on his belly in the underbrush, watching.

Jigger scooped out a last clod of dirt. Traggard then wedged the keg in the hole. It was a tight fit, and he had to wriggle the keg to make it fit. Drawing an Arkansas toothpick, Traggard chipped at the top of the keg. "We need a fuse," he said to Jigger. "Cut a strip from your shirt."

"Why mine?"

"Yours is wool. It will burn better than buckskin. Hurry it up, or I'll cut your shirt myself."

"Damnation, you're techy today," Jigger groused as he held the hem of his shirt in his left hand and slit into it with an antler-handled hunting knife.

"I don't like complications. If it wasn't for those damn dogs, we would have killed King and his friends from ambush and it would all be over except for collecting the money we'll be due."

"No one said anything about King owning hounds," mentioned the third killer. "How were we to know?"

"That's just it, Costa, we weren't," Traggard said. "It's a complication I can do without. Now, instead of rubbing them out the easy way, we have to do it the hard way." He tapped the keg. "Let's hope there's enough left of them that they can be identified."

"Strange we didn't see hide nor hair of his woman or his kids," Costa said. "He's supposed to have a girl about twelve and a son pushing twenty."

"One of the five men we saw was young enough to be the son," Traggard mentioned.

"But he sure didn't look like a 'breed." This from Jigger.

"Some 'breeds are more white than red," Traggard said. "And we didn't really get a good look at them, did we, thanks to those stinking dogs? As for King's squaw, she was probably inside cleaning or sewing or cooking. She just hasn't shown herself yet."

83

"Blowing this wall in should flush them out."

Costa said, "Ten thousand dollars is a lot of money." He was heavyset, but none of it was fat. Twin bushy sideburns reached to his lower jaw. "I'm glad it's not on my head."

"I found out about the bounty almost by accident," Traggard mentioned. "As it is, we got here first, but there are bound to be others."

The comment jolted Nate. He had not considered that. Even though it took weeks to reach the Rockies from Fort Leavenworth and even longer from places like St. Louis and New Orleans, and even though crossing the prairie was rife with peril, that much money would entice every cutthroat who heard of it. He *must* find out who was offering the bounty, and why, and put a stop to it.

"Will this do?" Jigger had cut a six-inch-by-two-inch strip from his shirt.

"Right fine, yes," Traggard complimented him. Taking the strip, he crimped one end and fed it into the hole in the top of the keg. "When I light it, we run for cover. Fetch some kindling." From an ammo pouch slanted across his chest he drew a fire steel and flint.

It was time for Nate to act. He started to rise but froze at the crunch of dry leaves. A bushy-bearded member of Traggard's gang was a few yards away, observing the preparations. So far Nate had gone unnoticed, but all bushy-beard had to do was turn in his direction and the man would see him. A shout or a shot, and the rest would come on the run.

Leaving the Hawken where it lay, Nate drew his

Bowie. Exercising extreme caution, he crab-slid to the right. None of the other cutthroats were anywhere near, that he knew of, but he did not rise into a crouch until he was directly behind bushy-beard, and when he did, he levered upward as if fired from a catapult. Clamping his left forearm across the man's throat to stifle any outcry, he plunged the Bowie into the man's back four times, one after the other, burying the blade to the Bowie's hilt between the man's shoulder blades.

At the first stab the man stiffened and opened his mouth, but no sound came out other than a bleat of astonishment. At the fourth thrust the man collapsed like a punctured water skin, and Nate quietly lowered him to the ground. The slight noise of the blade striking home had not been heard by the trio crouched by the cabin.

Swiveling right and left, Nate made sure no one else had witnessed the grisly deed. He never liked to kill, but he would do it when he had to, when it was necessary to safeguard those he loved, or, as in this instance, to prevent his cabin from being blown cloud-high, and the Stuarts along with it.

Retrieving the Hawken, Nate crept from tree to tree until he was behind a pine near the corral.

Jigger had gathered straw and made a small mound. Bent over it, Traggard was striking his fire steel against the flint to produce the spark that would ignite the straw and enable him to light the makeshift fuse.

Flattening, Nate crawled under the bottom rail. None of the three looked his way. Nor were there any shouts of warning from the woods as he rose in a crouch.

As the first spark flared, Nate was on them like an avenging Apache. Jigger saw him and tried to rise, but Nate slammed the Hawken against Jigger's head and, just like that, Jigger sprawled unconscious. Costa grabbed for a pistol and Nate did the same to him, hitting him so hard, Costa was slammed against the wall, his head cracking hard, like a chicken bone being snapped.

That left Lucian Traggard, who dropped the fire steel and flint and tried to rise while drawing a pistol.

Nate drove the Hawken's barrel into Traggard's gut and swore he could feel it glance off Traggard's spine. The man in green grunted and staggered but did not fall, only because Nate seized him by the shirt and shoved him toward the front of the cabin, saying, "Warn your men not to try anything. You die if they do."

Not giving Traggard time to yell or even think, Nate pushed him and held on to the back of the green buckskin shirt. Shouts of surprise rose from the forest and a rifle barrel poked from the vegetation.

"Don't shoot!" Traggard hollered. "Hold your fire! Do you hear me? That goes for all of you!"

Another rifle barrel appeared, but neither it nor the other spat lead.

Staying between Traggard and the wall, Nate sidled toward the door. As he went by the window, shards of glass all that remained of the costly pane, there were shouts of surprise from inside.

There were also shouts from the woods. "Don't shoot!" Traggard stressed. He did not sound scared; he did not look scared. He was merely doing what was necessary to stay alive.

"You're doing fine," Nate said, his fingers enfolded in the green buckskin shirt.

"Go to hell, whoever you are."

"Don't you recognize the man you came all this way to kill?" Nate could not resist the barb.

"You're Nate King?" Traggard exclaimed, and tried to twist to look at him. "That's not possible!"

Nate gouged the barrel into him, growling, "Eyes front!"

A few more steps brought them to the front door, which hung slightly ajar on leather hinges. Nate had replaced those hinges several times over the years, when they aged and cracked, the last time only a month ago. He kicked at the door and it swung all the way open.

Nate thought one of the Stuarts would be there to greet him, but it was a hound, its fangs bared, coiling to spring. He was about to strike it when Robert Stuart rushed up and grabbed the dog by the neck, bawling, "Heel, Hector! Heel!"

Immediately, the superbly trained animal stopped snarling and docilely let Stuart pull it aside.

Backing into the cabin, Nate gave Lucian Traggard a shove, then kicked the door shut.

"Nate! What in blazes are you doin' here?" Robert clapped him on the shoulder. "And who is your friend?" Robert blinked. "Why, if it isn't the gent who has been bellowin' at us for the past half an hour. Let me deal with the varmint." Robert's hand dropped to the hilt of his knife.

"We need him," Nate said, surveying the room. Four of the hounds, Hector now included, were over in a corner, sitting with their tongues hanging out. Two others were on their sides on the floor, one oozing blood from a bullet wound in the neck. The last was not breathing.

Arvil Stuart was next to the wounded hound, stroking it, and had tears in his eyes. "You'll be all right, Paris. Just hang on, boy."

Emory Stuart was on one side of the front window, Jethro Stuart on the other, their rifles cocked, ready to repel an assault. Over by the south wall sat Lee Stuart, his right shoulder stained red.

"The coyotes took us by surprise," Robert was saying. "They opened fire without so much as a word of warnin'. It's a miracle any of us made it inside alive." He grimly regarded Traggard. "This polecat was under the mistaken notion that one of us was you."

"So I've discovered," Nate said, and did what he had not had the opportunity to do outside; he relieved Traggard of a knife and two pistols and patted down the green buckskins to make sure Traggard did not have a concealed weapon up a sleeve or strapped under a pant leg.

"What's it all about?" Robert asked.

"That's what we're about to find out," Nate said, and roughly spun his prisoner around.

Lucian Traggard, oddly enough, was smiling as if

it were all a great joke and the joke was on them. "I won't tell you a damn thing."

"Think again," Nate said, and rammed the Hawken into the pit of the bounty killer's gut a second time. He wanted to hurt him and hurt him severely, and he did.

Doubled over in agony, spittle dribbling from his lower lip, Traggard wheezed, "You had no call to do that!"

"Says the man who came eighteen hundred miles to wipe out me and my family," Nate said coldly. He jerked a thumb at the window. "Yell to your men. Tell them not to fire or rush us. If they do, you'll be the first to die. I promise."

"And if I refuse?" Traggard defiantly demanded.

"The pain you're feeling now will be nothing compared to the pain I'll inflict next," Nate vowed, and hauled Traggard to the window so those lurking outside could see him. Nate drew his tomahawk. "What will it be?"

Traggard scowled but shouted, "Jigger, can you hear me?" When there was no answer, he shouted louder. "Jigger! Answer me, damn you!"

"He can't!" someone replied from out of the trees. "He was conked on the noggin and hasn't come around yet. What do you need, boss? It's me, Sprague."

"I know who it is, you yak!" Traggard yelled. "See to it that no one shoots or tries to get me out of here. Understood?"

"Sure, but is that wise? I mean, we can still blow the wall and rush them before they recover."

Traggard let out with a sigh. "It's so hard to find good help these days." To Sprague he said, "Don't do *anything*, damn your hide! Do you hear me? Sit tight and await instructions." As an apparent afterthought, he added, "Jigger is in charge once you revive him."

"Whatever you say," Sprague called. "But if they so much as lay a finger on you, give a holler!"

"Dumb but loyal," Traggard said to Nate. "Are you happy now? I've done as you wanted." He glanced at Robert Stuart. "So you really were telling the truth, after all? Who would have thought it?"

"Please let me shoot him," Robert requested.

Shaking his head, Nate shoved Traggard toward the north wall and pushed him to the floor. "Start talking."

"I'm still a bit rattled. Give me a minute."

Nate hit him. He slammed his fist against Traggard's right cheek, snapping Traggard's head half around. "The next one will be worse unless you cooperate."

Glowering and rubbing his cheek, Traggard rasped, "I'm beginning to understand why someone wants you dead."

"Who?"

"I have no idea."

Nate hit him again. Not once but three times, blows to the mouth and the jaw and the left ear. When he stepped back, Traggard was slumped against the wall, barely conscious, with blood trickling from a corner of his mouth. "I can keep this up all day if you make me."

"Let one of my hounds chew on him awhile," Robert Stuart suggested. "That will loosen his tongue."

It would be a few minutes before Traggard recovered enough to talk. Nate rested the Hawken's stock on the floor and leaned on it. "How bad off is your cousin?"

"The slug went clean through," Robert said. "Lee bled a lot, but it's stopped now." He smiled. "Thanks for askin'."

"Do you have any water to clean the wound?"

"Not so much as a thimbleful. All our water skins were on our horses, and our horses ran off."

Nate walked close to the front window but was careful not to show himself. "Sprague! Can you hear me?"

"This is Jigger," came an angry shout. "What's happening to Mr. Traggard in there?"

"I just beat him senseless," Nate said, "and I'll do worse if you don't bring a water skin to the front door. You have two minutes."

Lurid oaths blistered the air. "Whoever you are, mister, you'll rue this day. Honest to God you will."

"The water," Nate said, "or I start throwing your boss out in bits and pieces."

Emory Stuart whistled softly. "If you don't mind my sayin' so, Mr. King, you're a hellion with the bark on. I'm right proud to know you."

"If they don't give us the water," Jethro said, "I'll

91
.

gladly chop off that jasper's fingers and toes for you to toss out."

But Traggard's men complied. Jigger brought the water skin himself and set it down near the door. "Here you go! I hope you choke on every drop!"

Nate opened the door wide enough for Jigger to see Traggard, who was dazedly rubbing his chin. "He lives only so long as you do exactly as I say."

Jigger's face twitched as if he had been pricked with a pin. "Maybe we will and maybe we won't."

"Oh, you'll do it, all right." Nate played his ace. "Only Traggard knows how to get the bounty money. He dies, and you won't be paid a cent."

"How did you—?" Jigger began, and stopped. "You think you have us over a barrel. But it works both ways. Harm him, and we'll kill you out of sheer spite." His dark eyes glittering, he pivoted and stormed off.

Nate picked up the water skin and closed the door. He gave the skin to Robert, then hunkered in front of Lucian Traggard. "Ready to answer my questions?"

"Go to hell," Traggard snapped. "I already answered your first one, but you pounded on me anyway." He wiped a drop of blood from his lip. "I don't know who put up the bounty money. The lawyer never said."

"Lawyer?" Nate repeated.

"He practices law in New Orleans. Most of his clients are on the shady side of the law."

"Are you one of them?"

"No, but a friend of mine is. Denton mentioned

the bounty to me one day when we were talking about how we would like to have a lot of money. Denton is a gambler, and he said that if he had my experience in the woods, he would go after the bounty on a mountain man by the name of Nate King." Traggard's smile was vicious.

"So you have experience in the woods, do you?"

"For years I hunted gators for a living in the swamps. Sold their skins and their teeth and claws. It didn't make me rich, but I never starved, neither."

"And when you heard about the bounty, you figured you would take up hunting men instead."

"Why not? There's not much difference. Hunting is hunting. You track down what you're after, and it's over. I figured I had as good a chance as anyone else of claiming the ten thousand. Better, since I'm the first to come after you. I figured you wouldn't be expecting it." Lucian Traggard frowned at the hounds. "I never counted on something like this. Who the hell *are* these people, anyhow?"

"I ask the questions," Nate said. He had a lot of them. "Tell me about this lawyer. You went to see him?"

"Of course. I had to be sure the bounty offer was true. He's a nasty buzzard, that one. No qualms at all about having you and yours wiped out. Maybe that's why the person paying the bounty hired him."

Nate leaned forward. "Did he tell you who that person is?"

"He wouldn't say. I tried to get him to, but it's a condition of the bounty that the source of the money stay secret. Those were his exact words."

Traggard dabbed at another drop of blood. "Makes sense when you think about it. Whoever is after you doesn't want to get into hot water with the law."

Nate tried to think of an enemy who would go to such lengths. He had made more than a handful in his lifetime, but none were wealthy enough to offer a small fortune for his hide.

"Once I was sure the offer was genuine, I visited every tavern and grog shop along the waterfront looking for men with as few scruples as I have. It didn't take me long to find all I needed. And here we are."

Something occurred to Nate. "The lawyer never told you what I look like, did he? Or you would have known I wasn't here when you attacked."

Traggard sat straighter. "I'm no fool. Naturally, I asked him. He opened a wall safe and took out a letter or some other document and read it, then put it back in the safe and turned to me and said his client had not deigned to supply a description. Again, those were his exact words."

Could it be, Nate asked himself, that the lawyer's client had never met him? Is that why the lawyer had not supplied a description? Yet if they never met, why had the client posted the bounty? It made no sense.

"The only way for you to find out who is behind it is to go to New Orleans and have a talk with the lawyer."

Nate would rather jump off a cliff than journey east again. He'd had enough of civilization to last him the rest of his days.

"That's all I know, King. Except that once I brought back proof you and your family were dead, he was authorized to pay the ten thousand."

"What kind of proof?"

"He left that up to me. I was partial to taking your heads back, but he said that wasn't enough. I could kill any old family and claim it was yours, which I would do, too, if I thought I could get away with it. But I have to find papers and whatnot proving you're you. Any papers would do, even a family Bible if you have one."

Nate did, until all his books were destroyed. "What's the name of this lawyer?"

"Strange. I can't seem to remember." Traggard smirked. "So what now? Do you aim to kill me? Go right ahead. But my men will get you in the end."

Robert Stuart had been listening. "It will be dark in an hour or so, and I'll sic my hounds on them. By mornin' there won't be one of his maggots left alive."

Lucian Traggard looked at him. "Who in hell *are* you?"

"I'm no one," Robert said. "But I don't like it when someone tries to kill me. I don't like it one bit that you shot my cousin and killed one of my dogs and several of our horses. You have a lot to answer for."

"You'll lose a lot more before this is done," Traggard warned. To Nate he said, "Your best bet is to let me and the others go. My word of honor, we'll return to New Orleans and never bother you again."

Robert Stuart laughed. "Nate can speak for himself, but I wouldn't trust you as far as I can toss one of those mountains outside."

"No one asked you."

Nate didn't trust Traggard either. Not with ten thousand dollars at stake. There was only one way it would end, and they all knew what it was.

Just then Emory called to Robert from the window. "There's a commotion out yonder. They're up to somethin'."

"Let me," Nate said, rising. "You keep an eye on our guest."

A lot of yelling and the crackle of undergrowth confirmed that the bounty killers were moving about.

Nate caught a few snatches of what they were shouting and grinned. "It doesn't have to do with us. They just discovered I ran their horses off."

Emory Stuart chuckled. "You don't say? Then they're in the same predicament we are. We can use that to our advantage."

"I was thinking the same thing," Nate said.

A plan was taking shape. In a sense, Nate had been fortunate in that his loved ones were not there when Traggard's cutthroats struck. But when he did not return with Evelyn's horse by nightfall, his family and friends would worry, and one or more of them would come after him. He must dispose of the bounty men before then.

"For what it's worth, my kin and me will back you all the way," Emory mentioned. "No one shoots our dogs and gets away with it."

"They shot Lee, too," Nate noted. Jethro was over cleaning Lee's wound with water from the water skin.

"We're hill folk, Mr. King. Shootin' people is one thing. Shootin' a dog is as low as low can be. Out here they say that stealin' a horse can get a man shot. In the hills it's shootin' a man's dog. We're partial to our hounds. They're as much our family as our wives and kids." Emory glared out the window. "We owe these butchers."

"You'll get your revenge," Nate said. Depending on how his plan worked out, by the end of the night the bounty men would be dead, or they would.

Chapter Seven

Night had fallen and a myriad of stars sparkled in the vault of ink. In the distance wolves howled. To the northwest, a coyote yipped. Somewhere deep in the woods a deer bleated, followed seconds later by the snarl of frustration of a mountain lion that had misjudged its spring.

All these sounds and more Nate King heard as he leaned against the wall by the front window and waited with the patience of a hunter for the right moment to put his plan into effect. That moment came when off through the trees toward the lake a glow appeared. Small flames that rapidly grew into large flames. The bounty band had lit a campfire and were settling down. They would have men watching the cabin, but the night was moonless and it was now so dark, they would not be able to see their hands at arm's length.

"It won't be long," Nate commented.

In the dim gloom Nate could barely make out Emory Stuart, who was guarding Lucian Traggard. Earlier, Nate had bound Traggard's wrists behind his back using whangs from Traggard's green shirt.

Lee Stuart, his wound bandaged, was over with Arvil by the dogs. Jethro was at the door, which they had left open a crack.

"I still think we should all bust out at once," Robert Stuart said from the other side of the window. "They can't stop the six of us from reaching cover, and then we can fight them on our terms."

"I know what I'm doing," Nate said. Or he hoped he did. If it worked, they would be shed of the bounty men and his family would be safe. If it didn't work—he did not like to think of the consequences.

"It's your head the bounty is on," Robert said, "so we'll do it your way for now."

Hearing it said like that only made it that much harder for Nate to accept. Only the government put bounties on people, and he could not think of a single reason for the government to place one on him. It had to be someone else. A private party. But who?

Robert Stuart was having similar thoughts. "Any idea yet who might want you six feet under?"

"I'll sort it out eventually."

"You're taking it much more calmly than I would. Back in the hills, something like this would cause a blood feud that would last for generations."

"Oh, make no mistake. Whoever is to blame will pay," Nate vowed. "No one does this to a mountaineer with impunity."

"Is that what you call yourselves out here? Mountaineers?"

Nate was scouring the shrouded woods for clues to where those keeping watch were concealed. "It's what the early trappers called themselves. Nowadays, many call us mountain men."

"Which do you prefer?"

"A *free* man," Nate declared. "The mountains just happen to be here."

Robert's teeth were white in the dark. "You put a lot of store by bein' free, I take it?"

"More than anything," Nate admitted. Funny how that worked out. When he was growing up in New York, he always thought he *was* free. The newspapers extolled freedom to no end. The politicians liked to crow how free everyone was. Average citizens took great pride in being free.

It was only later, after Nate forsook New York for the frontier and had lived in the mountains for a while, that he realized those who lived east of the muddy Mississippi had no notion of what it meant to be truly free. True freedom did not involve being subject to hundreds of laws. True freedom did not involve having one's life dictated by those in political office. True freedom was not dependent on anyone or anything. It was a natural condition, a state of being as well as a state of mind, the state of being able to do whatever a person wanted when they wanted without let or hindrance.

Laws and rules were chains. They shackled people as surely as chains made of iron. It was always you couldn't do this or you shouldn't do that or you can't do the other thing no matter how much you wanted to.

Woe to anyone who dared to live truly free. Society did not abide those who broke its rules. Government came down hard on anyone who violated the law. An invisible leash was placed around everyone's neck the day they were born and kept there for the rest of their lives, and the punishment for trying to remove that leash was even less freedom.

The marvel of it to Nate was that people did not see the truth. Many, like his father, and like himself when he was younger, sincerely believed they enjoyed the true blessings of genuine freedom. All those laws? Why, they were necessary to preserve the public order. All those rules? Why, they were needed so society could run as smoothly as a clock. They were the foundations on which freedom rested. Or so was the common belief. But as in so many aspects of life, the common belief was not always how things truly and really were. More often than not, the common belief was a delusion.

Nate supposed that his first acquaintance with the idea of true freedom as opposed to artificial freedom was when he read the works of Thomas Paine. God, how he loved Paine. *These are the times that try men's souls* was as stirring a sentiment as was ever penned on paper. Even more than *Common Sense*; though Nate admired *The Rights of Man*. Who could read Paine's magnificent words and not be moved?

Some of the passages were indelibly impressed on his memory. *A great part of what is called govern-*

ment is mere imposition, Thomas Paine had written. *Government is no farther necessary than to supply the few cases to which society and civilization are not conveniently capable.* How eloquent, and how true. Yet how many people realized that? How many saw the danger in how powerful the government had become? And how that power diminished true freedom?

A copy of *The Rights of Man* had been one of Nate's favorite possessions. Many a night he had sat at the table and read from it by candlelight.

Thomas Paine had understood that government by its very nature imposed on freedom. *When extraordinary power and extraordinary pay are allotted to any individual in a government, he becomes the center, around which every kind of corruption generates and forms. Give to any man a million a year, and add thereto the power of creating and disposing of places, at the expense of a country, and the liberties of that country are no longer secure. What is called the splendor of a throne is no other than the corruption of the state. It is made up of a band of parasites living in luxurious indolence out of the public taxes.*

Worse, it resulted in more and more laws and less and less freedom, until citizens were slaves to the government that was supposed to serve them. Paine had seen the danger. Thomas Jefferson had seen it, too. So had George Washington. Why was it so few saw it now? Nate wondered.

Suddenly, Nate realized Robert Stuart was speaking to him.

". . . hear me? What are you doing, growin' roots?"

"I was thinking," Nate said.

"You do that a lot, I've noticed. I've never met anyone who spends as much time inside their head as you do."

"I'll take that as a compliment." Nate handed his Hawken to the Southerner. "Hold on to this, will you? It shouldn't take me more than half an hour."

"I should go with you."

"Two men make twice as much noise as one," Nate said. He started to turn, and paused. "Do me a favor. If something goes wrong, tell my wife I was thinking of her at the end."

"There you go again." Robert grinned. "Thinking."

Nate ducked under the window. He had removed the remaining shards of glass shortly after the sun went down. Now, gripping the sill with both hands, he tensed his entire body.

"Luck," Robert Stuart said.

Far off in the night, a mountain lion screeched.

Uncoiling, Nate vaulted up and over. He hoped that the lurkers in the trees were watching the door and not the window. Even if they were, the dark should screen him. His dive was clean and smooth. Tucking his chin to his chest, he landed on his shoulder and rolled up into a crouch. He awaited an outcry, but there was none. Confident he had gone unnoticed, Nate sidled along the front wall to the corner.

The night air was cool and bracing after the con-

fines of the cabin. The corral lay empty under the stars. He did not open the gate. Instead, as he had done once before, he crawled under the bottom rail and along the base of the south wall to the freshly dug hole. The keg of powder was still there.

Nate smiled. The bounty killers had made a mistake that would soon cost them. Gripping the keg with both hands, he lifted, but it was wedged fast. He remembered how Jigger had wriggled it to make it fit, and now he wriggled it to loosen it. The soft scraping sounds he made were not loud enough to carry to the trees. He tried lifting the keg out again, but it was still stuck. He wriggled it some more.

Nate was so focused on freeing the keg that movement in the corral registered belatedly. Letting go, he twisted just as a heavy form pounced. Hands seized his arms and other hands seized his neck. There were two of them, and they had been waiting for him. Traggard's men were smarter than he had given them credit for being, and now they had him. Or thought they did.

"Don't struggle and we won't hurt you, mister," one said. "We're to take you alive."

If that was supposed to convince Nate not to resist, it had the opposite effect. Like a mad bull, he heaved up off the ground, wrenching his right arm free as he rose. He clubbed the man who had hold of him by the neck and the man's hold slackened, but not enough for him to break loose. His other assailant was striving to clamp a hand on his wrist. Their combined weight caused Nate to trip and fall against the wall with a loud thump. He arced his knee up, and suddenly both his arms were free. Pivoting, he tossed one man over his hip.

Steel flashed in the starlight.

So much for them taking him alive, Nate thought, drawing his Bowie. He did not wait for them to come at him. He attacked, thrusting at the man who had drawn the knife. Metal rang on metal and the bounty killer backpedaled. The other one seized the moment and tried to tackle Nate about the ankles. A quick hop, and Nate was spared.

Every nerve tingling, Nate circled. In a knife fight it was suicide to stand still. He must keep moving, keep pressing. There might be more of them in the woods, but he did not let himself think about that. If there were, there was nothing he could do about it except resist them with steel and bullets.

His second assailant had drawn a knife. They were older than Traggard and Jigger, these two. In their forties, perhaps, seasoned veterans of the rough and violent world of New Orleans's underbelly.

"One last chance," said the second one. "Drop your pigsticker and we won't kill you."

"You have it backwards," Nate said.

They looked at each other, and the man who had spoken nodded. Then one came at Nate from the right and the other came at him on the left, darting in fast with their knives held as experienced knife fighters always held them, the blade tips midway between their waists and chests.

Nate parried, shifted, and countered a thrust at his neck. The blows were not delivered full force. His opponents were testing him, gauging his skill.

More proof they used their brains as well as their brawn. .

In the wilderness mistakes often proved deadly, and Nate had made a serious error in judgment. He had assumed that since they were city dwellers, Traggard's men would be easy to handle. He had met so many slow-witted, slothful products of civilization, he had forgotten civilization bred wolves, too. Tamer wolves than wilderness-bred wolves, but wolves nonetheless. Wolves who were clever and lethal and never, ever to be taken lightly.

They came at him again. Only now they were not testing him. They intended to end it quickly. One stabbed high, the other thrust low. Nate avoided both with a nimble sidestep. By now his back was to the woods and he was facing the cabin, and the short hairs on his neck prickled. But no shots shattered the quiet of the woodland. Apparently, there were only these two.

Nate skipped in close to one and the man nimbly skipped out of reach. The other one flicked his blade at Nate's arm, but Nate jerked aside.

The pale starlight had saved him several times; their blades glinted with every stroke, giving him a fraction's warning.

Then the unexpected occurred. A large cloud filled the sky above the corral, blotting out much of the starlight. Near-total blackness descended. All Nate could see was their vague shapes. He could not see their knives.

"At him!" one exclaimed, and both streaked in swift and furious.

GET
4 FREE BOOKS!

You can have the best Westerns delivered to your door for less than what you'd pay in a bookstore or online. Sign up for one of our book clubs today, and we'll send you **4 FREE* BOOKS**, worth $23.96, just for trying it out...**with no obligation to buy, ever!**

———◆◆◆———

Authors include classic writers such as
LOUIS L'AMOUR, MAX BRAND, ZANE GREY
and more; PLUS new authors such as
COTTON SMITH, TIM CHAMPLIN, JOHNNY D. BOGGS
and others.

———◆◆◆———

As a book club member you also receive the following special benefits:
- **30% OFF** all orders through our website & telecenter!
- **Exclusive access** to special discounts!
- **Convenient** home delivery and **10 days to return any books you don't want to keep.**

There is no minimum number of books to buy,
and you may cancel membership at any time.
See back to sign up!

*Please include $2.00 for shipping and handling.

YES! ☐

Sign me up for the Leisure Western Book Club
and send my FOUR FREE BOOKS! If I choose to stay
in the club, I will pay only $14.00* each month,
a savings of $9.96!

NAME: _____

ADDRESS: _____

_____

TELEPHONE: _____

E-MAIL: _____

☐ I WANT TO PAY BY CREDIT CARD.

☐ VISA ☐ MasterCard. ☐ DISCOVER

ACCOUNT #: _____

EXPIRATION DATE: _____

SIGNATURE: _____

Send this card along with $2.00 shipping & handling to:

Leisure Western Book Club
20 Academy Street
Norwalk, CT 06850-4032

Or fax (must include credit card information!) to: 610.995.9274.
You can also sign up online at www.dorchesterpub.com.

*Plus $2.00 for shipping. Offer open to residents of the U.S. and Canada only.
Canadian residents please call 1.800.481.9191 for pricing information.
If under 18, a parent or guardian must sign. Terms, prices and conditions subject to change. Subscription subject
to acceptance. Dorchester Publishing reserves the right to reject any order or cancel any subscription.

JOIN NOW!

Nate retreated, keeping enough space between him and their blades that they could not connect. It worked for all of ten seconds. Then his back came up against the rails and he could not retreat any further.

"We have him!"

Nate feinted right but went left. He heard the swish of metal on air. Something tugged at the whangs on his sleeve but did not sink into his flesh. Turning so the pair were in front of him, he awaited their next rush.

Impatience in a fight was the worst lapse of all. A man must stay calm. He must think clearly and rationally without really thinking, if that made sense.

The heavier of Nate's adversaries forgot that important fact. "Damn you!" he hissed in frustration, and hurled himself forward, intent on overpowering Nate by sheer brutish force.

"No, Abner!" the other cried.

In the blackness it was doubtful Abner saw Nate's Bowie. He most certainly felt it, though, when the big blade sheared between his ribs and buried itself in his torso. He most certainly felt the pain and the sticky, wet, warm sensation of his life's blood. Neither the pain nor the sensation of the blood lasted long, because the Bowie had pierced his heart and Abner died with a strangled grunt and a gasp.

Pulling the Bowie out, Nate avoided the falling body and confronted the remaining killer.

"Abner was my friend," the man said.

Nate felt no sympathy whatsoever. These men had come to murder him and his loved ones. To murder his wife of many years, and his daughter, a girl who never harmed a soul in her life. These men deserved to die, by any means necessary.

"My name is Ira. Ira Stimms. I want you to know it, mister. I want you to know the name of the man who does you in." His left hand streaked to his belt.

Nate had sensed what the other was about to do a split second before Stimms did it. Knives had not worked, so the logical thing to do was resort to a gun. That they had not done so sooner was a blunder on their part, motivated by their wish to take him alive and perhaps by a desire not to alert those in the cabin to what was going on. But Ira Stimms no longer cared. Stimms would shoot him and be done with it.

A full-size flintlock was not light. Stimms could not draw it as swiftly as the situation called for. He had it half out when Nate drove the Bowie into his stomach with the blade angled up, and twisted.

"Oh, God!" Stimms blurted. His knife fell, and he let go of the pistol and clutched Nate's forearm. "Oh God, oh God, oh God, oh God."

Nate yanked the Bowie out and stepped back.

Splaying his hands over the gaping wound, Stimms tottered. "This can't be happening! You've done killed me."

Nate broke his long silence. "In your next life, maybe you'll think twice before you hire on to murder innocents."

"My next one?" Ira Stimms said, and ended this one with a pitiable whimper and a sob.

Nate hunkered and regarded the wall of vegetation. No one had come to the aid of the pair in the corral. They were clever but they were careless, these hired assassins, and their carelessness would be their undoing.

He wiped his Bowie clean on Stimms's shirt and hurried to the cabin. A few jabs with the Bowie and he loosened the dirt enough for him to lift the keg from the hole. The makeshift fuse flopped against the side.

With the keg under his left arm, Nate climbed over the rails and padded into the forest. To the east danced the reddish-orange flames of the campfire, a beacon that brought him to a cluster of small pines only a stone's throw from the cutthroats who sought his life.

Eight mercenaries ringed the fire. Jigger was there, pouring coffee into a tin cup. Costa was there, too, his chin in his hands.

"You should go dip your head in the lake if it hurts so much," another man was commenting. "The cold water will help ease the pain."

"I've already done it four times," Costa said woefully. "I'm half waterlogged."

"We owe that big bastard," Jigger growled. "Before it was business. Now it's personal."

"I wonder who wants King dead, and why?" asked a fourth man.

"Who cares? When you're hired to kill a man, Wallace, you don't question the motive. You just do it, like you would kill a fly or a bird or any other critter."

"Flies and birds aren't people, Jigger. It might be

easy for you, but some of us have a shred of conscience left."

"Then you shouldn't have hired on. A conscience is for parsons, Bates, not those who make their living by breaking the law day in and day out."

"All I'm saying—" Bates began.

Jigger held up a hand. "Save your prattle. And before I forget, along about midnight you and Wallace relieve Ira and Abner."

"Why us?"

"Why not you?"

Bates pulled a pocket watch from his vest and opened it. "We have a couple of hours yet. Pass me some jerky."

Another man had an open saddlebag next to his legs, and he reached in and brought out a piece of jerked venison. "Here you go."

"A hell of a thing, we can't shoot game," Bates said. "It's not as if King and his friends don't know we're here."

"You can eat a hot meal when Traggard is safe, not before," Jigger said.

"You've sure gotten bossy."

The short man put his hands on his hips. "He put me in charge, if you'll recollect. So quit your bellyaching. You're just jealous he didn't pick you."

"That's ridiculous, Jigger," Bates said, but his tone suggested maybe it wasn't. He bit into the jerky and gloomily chewed.

Jigger stared toward the trail to the cabin. "One of us should go check that everything is all right."

"If they weren't, Stimms or Abner would holler," Bates said.

"Go anyway."

"Me? What are you picking on me for? I'm eating. Choose someone else."

"I picked you, Bates," Jigger said.

The pair did not like each other, that much was obvious. Tension crackled in the air, and several of the others edged back in case Jigger or Bates went for their pistols.

"On your way," Jigger commanded.

Bates set down his tin cup so violently he spilled some coffee. "When this is over and we're back in New Orleans, you and me will have a talk."

"I can't wait."

Nate hadn't counted on this. He intended to wait until they were asleep, then roll the keg into the fire and run. The blast should deal with most of them, and those who were left, he would tend to personally.

Biting into the jerky, Bates rose and hitched at his belt. "Don't think I won't tell Traggard how you've treated me, because I will." He picked up a rifle.

"Good. Lucian will enjoy the laugh." Jigger waggled a hand. "Off you go. And try not to trip and fall on your face."

"I'll take a brand," Bates said, and reached for the unlit end of a burning log.

"You'll do no such thing" was Jigger's sharp reply. "Not unless you want those in the cabin to take a shot at you."

111

Costa spoke up. "If you're afraid of the dark, Bates, I'll go with you and hold your hand."

They all laughed except Bates. Muttering, he wheeled and stalked toward the trail.

Nate had to stop him. But he could not do it close to the fire. Leaving the keg under a pine, he crawled backwards until it was safe, then rose and angled through the trees to intercept his quarry. Midway to the cabin, he flattened and drew the Bowie.

Bates was taking his sweet time.

Nate heard the man still muttering as Bates came around a bend. Coiled to pounce, Nate was taken aback when Bates unexpectedly stopped.

Someone was coming down the trail from the opposite direction. From the cabin. Bates snapped his rifle to his shoulder and barked, "Who's there? Identify yourself or I'll shoot!"

A shambling figure lurched out of the night. "It's me!" Ira Stimms croaked, his arms over his midriff. "I've been cut to pieces."

Nate could scarcely credit his senses. Then he remembered. He had not checked for a pulse. Neither Stimms nor the other one, Abner. He had assumed they were dead, and now his oversight had cost him.

"What's that? Who cut you, Ira?"

Stimms's intestines were oozing between his fingers. "It was King," he huffed. "He's out here somewhere. Warn the others."

Nate started to rise, but Bates had whirled and was flying toward the lake, bawling at the top of his lungs. Blowing them up with the powder had to wait. He turned toward the cabin, only to find his way blocked by a hideously pale apparition.

"You!" Ira Stimms shrieked.

The man was dead on his feet. Nate swerved to go around him, but Stimms took a lurching step and wrapped gore-caked arms around his neck.

"Here! He's here! I've got Nate King! Come quick!"

Nate sought to wrest loose, but Stimms clung tenaciously on, all the while hollering for help. Voices sounded, and a rush of footfalls. "Damn you!" Nate said, and finished what he had started by sinking the Bowie into Stimms's chest. This time there was no doubt.

Pushing the body off, Nate sought to escape. But somehow Stimms had locked his fingers and Nate could not pry Stimms's arms off. Weighted down, Nate took a few steps, when without warning the darkness disgorged half a dozen figures who swarmed on him like berserk demons.

Chapter Eight

Nate King speared his Bowie at the first assailant to rush out of the night, only to have another swing a rifle and catch him across the elbow, deflecting the blow and rendering his entire arm numb. He lost his hold on the Bowie's hilt. Before he could bend to retrieve it or draw a pistol, the rest were on him; he was buried under a thrashing, kicking, pummeling avalanche.

Nate fought back with a savagery born of that most basic of human instincts—self-preservation. He punched, he kicked, he bucked, he laid about him with his fist like a madman, raining lightning blows that jarred his attackers. But there were too many. For every bounty killer he knocked down, another instantly took the man's place. For every one of his blows that connected, four or five of theirs landed solidly on him.

He thought for sure they would stab him or shoot

him until he heard someone—Jigger—shout over the bedlam of close combat.

"Don't kill him! Don't kill him!"

Nate had no chance to wonder why they wanted him alive. Not that it changed anything. He had to break free and make it back to the cabin.

It was eight against one, though—seven, actually, since Jigger did not take part but pranced about at the fringe of the melee exhorting the others over and over not to kill him—and although Nate was bigger than any of them and twice as strong as any one of them, the best he could do was delay the inevitable.

Nate's right fist connected with a jaw. His left clipped an ear. He kicked Costa where it hurt any man the worst, and was in turn kicked by someone else in the same spot. Pain exploded in his groin. The night sky swirled and changed places with the ground. Then there were three of them on his chest and others pinned his arms and legs. Although he exerted every sinew to its fullest, more than he had exerted himself ever, he could not throw them off. A shape flitted out of the dark and loomed over him in triumph.

"We did it! We got him!" Jigger cried.

"We?" Bates said breathlessly.

Unruffled, Jigger declared, "This couldn't have worked out better if I planned it." His right arm seemed to grow longer. A pistol blossomed in Nate's face. "I thank you for being so considerate."

"Go to hell," Nate said, unsure what the other meant.

"One day, no doubt," Jigger said. Then the arm that had grown longer rose on high and descended.

Once, twice, three times molten agony coursed through Nate's head. He fought to stay conscious, but the pistol Jigger was using was a lot harder than his skull. The stars blurred, then the forest went black and he felt sick to his stomach just before everything faded, even Jigger's sadistic laugh.

Nate had never been stomped to death in a stampede, but he could have sworn that was what had happened to him when consciousness returned with startling clarity. He was aware of lying on his back with his ankles and wrists bound. He was aware of the snap and pop of a blazing fire, and the low murmur of voices. But most of all, he was aware of the pain. Total, near-overwhelming pain. Pain in every inch of his body. His head throbbed and his left cheek throbbed, and his ribs were not ribs at all but instruments of the most excruciating torture.

"I think the mountain man is awake," someone said.

"How can you tell?" Bates asked. "His face is so swollen he looks like a pumpkin."

"His isn't the only one," Costa said.

"So you have a nasty bump or two?" Jigger interposed. "You're better off than Traggard. There's no telling what they've done to him."

Nate opened his eyes and was seized by panic. *They had blinded him! Everything was black as pitch!* Then colors swirled into bright focus and through puffy eyelids he saw Jigger standing over him, holding the very pistol Jigger had beaten him senseless with.

"Damn me if you don't look like a pumpkin! A black-and-blue pumpkin with mashed lips and a bloody nose and a split ear."

"Why—?" Nate asked, but could say no more. His mouth would not work as it should.

Jigger understood. "Why are you still alive after what you've done? Because I need you for the swap."

Bates snapped his fingers. "Oh. I get it. You're going to trade King for Traggard. But will those bastards inside go along?"

"His wife and kids won't want any harm to come to him," Jigger predicted. "They'll agree, sure enough."

"Strange we haven't seen any sign of the squaw or his son or daughter yet," Wallace mentioned.

A loud groan sounded, but not from Nate. He started to twist his head to find the source and nearly passed out from the pounding waves of torment the slight movement provoked.

Jigger swiveled on the balls of his feet. "Ira, you have to stop doing that. It's getting on my nerves."

"Leave him be," Bates said. "He's dying, for God's sake."

"He can have the decency to die quietly," Jigger snapped, "and not impose his suffering on the rest of us."

"I hope you suffer when your time comes. I hope you go through exactly what poor Ira is going though."

"I'd cork that mouth of yours, Bates. There is only so much guff I'll abide." Jigger held the flint-lock menacingly. "And I have abided my limit."

A man in a river rat's cap spat a wad of tobacco. "Hold on there, you two. Let's not squabble amongst ourselves. Traggard wouldn't like it. And it's a long ride back across that prairie, with Injuns everywhere."

"Injuns, hell," Wallace said. "We didn't see a single redskin all the way here. If you ask me, those stories about folks being scalped are tall tales."

"Just because a person has never been burned doesn't mean fire ain't hot," another bounty man said.

"Now, that there was a damned intelligent comment," Jigger said. "How do you come up with them, Sprague?"

"Why, being smart just sort of comes to me."

Jigger uttered twenty cusswords in half as many seconds, ending with. "Idiots. I am up to my neck in idiots. No wonder Traggard made me second-in-command." He jabbed a dirty fingernail at Sprague. "If brains were gold, you would be dirt poor." He jabbed the same finger at Wallace. "We didn't see any buffalo, either, but that doesn't mean buffalo don't exist." Again he jabbed his finger, this time at the man in the river rat's cap. "And when it comes to squabbling, Traggard puts up with even less than I do." He turned back to Nate. "As for you, you can lie there and hurt like hell until morning. If you get thirsty, tough. If you want something to eat, too bad. But by all means feel free to ask, so I can laugh in your face."

Costa grinned. "You sure beat all, Jigger."

Nate forced his mouth to work.

"What's that?" Jigger bent down. "You'll have to speak up. I can't hear you when you whisper."

"You are all dead," Nate said.

Jigger blinked, then cackled. "Amazing. Plumb amazing. Beaten to a pulp and trussed like a lamb for slaughter, and *you* threaten *us*? Like I said, I am surrounded by idiots."

Nate did not say more. He couldn't. It had drained him as if he had run ten miles. He closed his eyes and shut his ears to the hubbub of conversation and soon drifted into a semiconscious limbo of past memories and present pain. When he opened his eyes again, by the position of the Big Dipper it was past midnight. His throat was abominably dry and his mouth felt like it was filled with sand. He gazed longingly toward the lake and imagined sinking onto his hands and knees and drinking cool, refreshing water until he was fit to burst, but the imagining made him thirstier, so he stopped and gazed toward the fire instead.

The flames had burned low. All the killers save two were asleep. One was the man called Sprague, who had a rifle between his legs. The other was Jigger, nursing a cup of coffee.

"So you're back with the living again?"

Nate did not try to speak.

"I bet you'd like a drink right about now," Jigger

119

said, grinning. "Sprague, give him a drink from your cup."

"What?"

"Are you hard of hearing as well as brainless? Give the man a drink."

"But earlier you said not to. You said that if any of us so much as looked at him, you would shoot us."

"That was then and now is now," Jigger said impatiently. "Give him a drink, you sack of mule droppings, before I come over there and beat you with a rock."

Sprague set down his rifle. "All right, all right. You don't have to talk so mean to everybody, you know. We're on your side, remember? It wouldn't hurt you to be nice just once."

"The only side I'm on is my own," Jigger said. "And in this world being nice can get you buried. So I'll stay as I am, thank you very much."

From a sack next to a saddle Sprague took a tin cup. "I don't see why Traggard thinks so highly of you."

"I don't take kindly to insults," Jigger warned. "But just so you know, he relies on me because I always get the job done no matter what the job is. I don't have scruples, like some of you misfits. I don't have a conscience that nags me to tears. I'd kill my own mother if someone paid me enough."

"You're despicable," Sprague said. "I don't care if that makes you mad or not. I've killed, plenty of times, but I'd never stoop that low."

"Fetch the water while you still can."

"Save your threats. You won't shoot me. You

need me to help deal with those men in the cabin."
Smugly smirking, Sprague ambled toward the lake.

"Did you hear him?" Jigger asked, but he was
not addressing Nate. He was talking to himself.
"Before we reach New Orleans he's going to have
an accident. I can guarantee."

Nate was not bloodthirsty by nature. He seldom
wanted to rub anyone out, but he would not hesitate to rub out the embodiment of hate across the
fire from him. Jigger was a festering sore who
spread violence like rats spread the plague, and
who would not stop festering this side of the
grave.

The scruffy killer was studying him. "I should
thank you, mister. The more of us you kill, the
more money there is for the rest." He waited as if
for a reply, then said, "Cat got your tongue? Well,
you'll talk in a bit."

It was a veiled threat. Nate met the other's gaze
and forced his mouth to quirk in a defiant sneer.

Jigger chuckled. "I admire you, King. I truly do.
Anyone who can be beaten to a pulp and not break
has to be made of iron."

The flattery rang false on Nate's ears.

"What we're doing, it's nothing personal, you
understand? We're doing it for the money."

That was supposed to soothe his outrage? Nate
let his sneer widen.

"I don't blame you for feeling like you do. I
would feel the same if I were in your moccasins. I
wouldn't want my family to die, either. But if they
had to die, and yours do, then I'd want them to die

quick and not suffer." Jigger paused. "Do you want your family to suffer?"

Nate flexed his arms, but his captors had done a good job. He could not break free.

"Why not make it easy on yourself and on them?" Jigger asked. "Why not have them come out with their hands in the air? I promise they won't suffer. A shot to the head and it will be over."

The man was unbelievable, Nate reflected.

"Something for you to think about," Jigger said. "Ah. Here's that water. Give it to him."

Sprague had been about to hand the tin cup to Jigger. Frowning, he sank onto a knee and slid a hand under Nate's head to raise it high enough for Nate to drink. "I don't see why I have to do all this," Sprague groused.

"Because I say so," Jigger said.

The water was wonderful. Nate wished there were a gallon of it. His mouth and throat were no longer parched, but he was still thirsty. He was also famished. But he would not let on. He would not show weakness.

"There. Isn't that better?" Jigger asked when the cup was drained and Sprague had returned it to the pack.

"Want me to roast some venison for him, too?" Sprague asked tartly.

"No. I want you to go check on the cabin."

"What for? Bates and Wallace are up there. They'll give a yell if those inside try anything."

"I wouldn't put it past either of those lunkheads

122

to sleep instead of keeping watch." Jigger impatiently motioned. "Off you go."

Sprague angrily snatched up his rifle and stomped toward the trail. "Do this! Do that! I'll be glad when Traggard is back in charge."

Jigger took the coffeepot from a flat rock near the fire and refilled his cup. Settling on his haunches, he slowly sipped while eyeing Nate. "Now that I've done you a favor, how about you do me one?"

"Cut me free and we'll talk about it," Nate said.

Jigger laughed, then shook his head. "You stay tied until we make the swap in the morning. In the meantime, I want to know who wants you dead."

"That makes two of us."

"Come on. You must know. A complete stranger wouldn't pay so much money for your hide. Give me a name."

"I don't have one."

"I don't believe you." Jigger sipped again, his eyes hooded. "I believe you know and you're keeping it to yourself. But it's important to me I find out. Important enough that you don't want to make me mad."

"If I knew, I would say." After all, Nate mused, what difference did it make?

Jigger did not seem to hear him. "Maybe you think that by keeping it a secret you can somehow protect your family. But you're only making it worse for them. Because if you don't tell me, I'll get the information from one of them. One way or the other."

"I don't know, I tell you," Nate said earnestly.

"Sure, sure. But I need to know. Are you paying attention? I *need* to know. It is of the utmost importance."

"Why?" Nate asked, and even as he did, the answer occurred to him. If Jigger could find out who was paying the bounty, Jigger wouldn't need Traggard. Jigger would not need any of his fellow bounty men. Sprague was not the only one who would suffer an "accident." Jigger would reach New Orleans alone, and claim all the money for himself.

"I did you a favor by giving you that water. Now repay the courtesy and tell me who it is."

"I wish to God I did know."

"Suit yourself, mountain man," Jigger said. "Just remember what I said about your family. They'll suffer for your pigheadedness."

"What would Traggard say about your interest in the source of the bounty money?" Nate resorted to a veiled threat of his own.

"Why bring him into it? This is between you and me." Jigger tried to appear unruffled by the question, but he failed.

After that, the unkempt killer said no more, not even when Sprague came back to report it was quiet at the cabin.

Nate tried to sleep. His badly battered body needed the rest. But though he shut his eyes and willed himself to relax and tried not to dwell on the pain or his plight, he could not doze off. His mind was to blame. His thoughts raced with lightning swiftness and with exceptional clarity. He realized that Jigger's devious scheme would succeed. The Stuarts would agree to a swap to save his life. Robert Stuart was no fool, though, and would demand that it be done in such a manner as to forestall treachery. Jigger would agree, but that in itself was part of the deception. For as surely as Nate was still alive, Jigger would contrive to slay him and the Stuarts, and do it in such a way that the Stuarts would be dead before they knew what was what.

How would Jigger go about it? That was the question. Nate pondered long and hard, and although he came up with four or five possible ways, they were too obvious. Robert Stuart was not likely to fall for them.

Nate could not divine the twisted depths to which Jigger might go.

Then, too, Nate had another worry, a worry that gnawed at him like termites at wood, the worry that some of his loved ones would come looking for him. By now Winona knew something was wrong. He hoped she would wait until morning to search for him, and would not come alone. But it could well be—and this was what worried him the most—it could well be that she had set out, alone, well before sunset, and if she did not stop for the night, if she was so anxious for his welfare that she pushed on, she might at that very moment be nearing the cabin, unaware of the peril that awaited her.

Fear filled Nate at the mere thought. He could bear any danger to himself. He could endure any threat to his own life, usually with a calmness that surprised him. Perhaps because he had been in danger so many times, he had learned to cope with crises without losing his head. But he could not bear the idea of harm befalling those he cared for. He could not endure threats to Winona or Zach or Evelyn or any of his dearest and nearest friends.

His fear inspired Nate to a desperate act. He could not lie there and do nothing. In a few hours, the sun would rise. He must thwart whatever vicious ploy Jigger had in mind. And in the process, ensure that Winona would not be in danger when she showed up.

But what to do? How to free himself? Nate twisted his wrists back and forth to loosen the whangs, but after five minutes all he had succeeded in doing was rubbing his skin raw. Whoever tied him had tied them sadistically tight. So tight that although his wrists bled and the blood made the whangs as slick as if they were coated with grease, he could not slip loose no matter how he tugged and pulled.

At last Jigger put down his tin cup and turned in.

Only Sprague was awake, keeping watch, and he was so drowsy he repeatedly yawned and shook himself.

Nate lay with his face to the fire, his eyes open the barest crack. He had not moved in a long time, except for secretly working at his bounds to give Sprague the impression he was asleep. Evidently, it had worked.

Sprague was not paying any attention to him. Soon Sprague's eyelids drooped shut. Almost immediately, Sprague jerked his head up and blinked. Struggling to stay awake, he stretched and moved his legs, but soon his eyelids were drooping again. A second time he jerked awake. But only temporarily. He would doze off, then snap awake, doze off, then snap awake. Seven or eight times it happened, and each time his eyes stayed shut for longer and longer intervals. Then came the moment Nate was waiting for: Sprague's eyes closed and stayed closed, and Sprague slumped against his saddle, sound asleep.

Jigger was snoring. None of the others had stirred in hours.

Nate's chance had come. By levering on his elbow and his knees, he inched toward the fire. At any instant, any of the killers might awaken. Whenever one stirred or muttered, Nate froze.

The fire was slowly going out. The few flames were three or four inches high. The heat from the embers, though, was considerable. Nate felt it when he rolled onto his side so his back, and his bound wrists, were to the flames. Carefully extending his arms, he winced when fire seared his left hand.

Craning his neck so he could see his wrist, Nate shifted so the flames licked at the whangs. Unfortunately, they were so tight, he could not burn through them without burning himself. Gritting his teeth, he thrust his wrists into the fire. He would char his forearms black if he had to.

The odor of burnt buckskin mixed with that of burnt flesh, a pungent scent that once smelled was never forgotten.

Pain rippled up Nate's arms in waves. Pain so intense he nearly blacked out. Sweat beaded his forehead and dripped into his eyes, stinging terribly. His fingers grew numb, but whether from having his circulation cut off or from the flames, he could not say.

Over and over Nate tried to snap the whangs. They were bound to weaken eventually. All he had to do was withstand the pain until they did. But it grew worse and worse until it eclipsed all else. He heard his skin sizzling. He smelled his own blood. And just when he thought he could not stand it anymore, he strained his wrists yet one more time and the whangs parted with a snap.

Without thinking, Nate swung both arms around in front of him. The torment was excruciating. For a few seconds Nate was under the illusion that his arms had been torn from their sockets. His senses swam in a sea of blinding-white agony. Involuntarily, he gasped, then stiffened and looked right and left, certain one or more of the sleepers would awaken. But none of them did, although Ira Stimms moaned and mumbled and pink froth trickled from a corner of his mouth.

Nate pulsed with anguish. He held his arms still, but when the pain did not subside fast enough to suit him, he quietly sat up and bent to untie the whangs binding his ankles. It was a mistake. His circulation had been cut off for so long, every nerve screamed in protest.

Chafing with irritation at being unable to do as he so desperately needed to do, Nate bowed his head to his knees. It would not be long, he assured himself. A minute or two at the most. He flexed his fingers. He twisted his wrists from side to side. He raised his shoulders, one and then the other, relying on movement to restore the use of his limbs that much sooner.

Suddenly, Ira Stimms moaned louder than ever before. Stimms's eyes opened and his head turned directly toward Nate. His mouth parted, and Nate braced for an outcry. Instead, Stimms sucked air into his lungs, exhaled loudly, and was still. The man had finally died.

With great effort, Nate rose to his knees. The dark woods beckoned. There he would be safe from the bounty pack until dawn. But it would be folly to go unarmed. He needed weapons, preferably his own. He saw his tomahawk beside a sleeping figure and moved toward it.

At that juncture fate intruded, but not in a manner Nate anticipated. The smell of his blood and burning flesh had attracted a roving predator. Out of the vegetation lumbered one of the ursine lords of the Rockies, a grizzly bear in all its formidable might. And at sight of him and the camp, the great bear opened its razor-rimmed maw and roared.

Chapter Nine

In the dark Nate King could be forgiven his mistake. The bear was so big that anyone might have assumed it to be a grizzly. But as it shambled into the ring of light cast by the fading fire, the absence of a hump revealed the truth: It was a black bear.

In the normal course of events, black bears were seldom dangerous. They preferred to go the other way at the sight or scent of a human. But there were exceptions to every rule, and this particular black bear was one of them. Instead of fleeing, it had come to investigate the scents its sensitive nose had detected on the night wind. Why it roared was a mystery only the black bear could explain.

For Nate, all that mattered was that Jigger and Sprague and Costa and Evans and the rest of the bounty band did what any man would do under like circumstances. At the bear's outburst, they scrambled from under their blankets, yelling and glancing every which way in confusion, seeking the cause of that which had startled them from their sound slumber.

The confusion bought Nate the precious seconds he needed. As the black bear approached the fire from the north and became the focus of attention for the pack of man-killers, Nate reared erect and bolted toward the woods to the west. Lurched would be a more accurate description, for he found, to his dismay, that the circulation in his legs had also been cut off and now they would not move as fast nor as smoothly as he would like them to move. He willed them to take long, quick steps, but the best he could manage were short steps with a ponderous slowness that made his recapture virtually inevitable.

Frustration tore at Nate like a saber. To be so close to escaping, and then be thwarted by his own limbs! He wished he had been able to grab a weapon so he could give a good account of himself when they jumped him.

"What the hell? What the hell?" Sprague bawled.

"It's a bear!" Costa added to the general din.

Several of the Easterners snapped rifles to their shoulders or took aim with pistols, but Jigger kept his wits about him, and bellowed, "Don't shoot unless I say to! Do you hear me?"

The black bear had stopped a dozen feet from the fire and was loudly sniffing while regarding the two-legged intruders intently.

All of which Nate took in at a glance. Only a little farther to the woods and he would be safe!

"What does the critter want?" Sprague wondered in high-pitched panic. "What if it attacks us?" He nervously fingered the trigger of his rifle.

"Don't fire, damn your yellow hide!" Jigger fumed. "It might let us be without lifting a paw if we let it be."

"It's so big!" another man marveled. "Look at the size of that thing!"

Many people did not appreciate how truly immense bears grew. Up close they were positively terrifying. They had been to Nate, years ago, before he encountered so many that his fear wore off and he began to regard them as nuisances rather than monsters. Not that he ever took bears lightly. Grizzly or black, they were the most unpredictable predators on God's teeming earth, and armed as they were with strong teeth and long claws, they were bestial killing machines, or the closest thing to it, as unstoppable in their way as steam engines.

Nate's legs were responding. He was moving a little faster.

The backs of all the killers were to him; they were glued to the bear, which had reared on its hind legs and was still nosily sniffing.

Bears relied on their noses much as humans relied on sight, and this one was apparently unsure whether it had stumbled on prey or should run.

Nate plunged into the vegetation. The instant he was out of sight, he veered toward the cabin. The Stuarts had spare weapons, and water and food besides.

A glance showed Nate that the bear had dropped

onto all fours. Suddenly, it grunted. Wheeling, it raced off with a speed that belied its bulk. Another few moments and it barreled into the forest, departing as noisily as it had arrived.

"There it goes!" Sprague exclaimed in relief. "We scared it off!"

"We were lucky," Jigger said. He lowered his rifle and turned and reacted as if he had been slapped. "Hey! Where in hell did King get to?"

"He's gone!"

"I can see that, jackass!" Jigger galvanized into angry motion. "What are all of you waiting for? An engraved invitation? *Find him*, you miserable laggards! Find the damn mountain man and fetch him back so we can trade him for Lucian Traggard!"

It was a marvel how men twice Jigger's size leaped to obey his commands as if he were the Almighty incarnate.

Bent at the waist, Nate moved as swiftly as the darkness permitted. He hurt all over. He had so many bruises, scrapes and wounds that there wasn't a part of his body not in pain. Pain he shut from his mind as he glided through the benighted forest with the deceptive ease of a prowling panther. He could not shut it out completely, though. Now and again it made its presence known.

The undergrowth crackled to the passage of his pursuers.

Nate had a big enough lead that he was confident they would not spot him. But he left nothing to chance, and when he came to a log overgrown by high weeds, he flattened next to it and pulled the weeds over him, bending the stems so they formed a canopy, effectively shielding him from casual scrutiny.

The bounty men had spread out and were moving abreast. Some beat the brush with rifle barrels. Others thrust at the weeds and thickets with long knives.

Costa came near the log and was joined by Sprague. Both were so close, Nate could stretch out an arm and touch them. But the inky veil of night protected him with its mantle.

"It's like looking for a needle in a haystack," Sprague complained.

"Go tell Jigger," Costa said, "and I'll bury you deep so the coyotes don't dig up your remains."

"I'm not scared of him," Sprague said, but it was as plain as his weasel features that he was lying.

"So long as we're facing him, we're safe enough," Costa said. "It's when we turn our backs to him he's most liable to strike."

"I've felt uneasy ever since we reached these mountains," Sprague remarked. "There's something about them. Like when I'm out in the Gulf of Mexico on a boat and I see a thunderhead far off. Or that night I spent at a haunted house."

"In a what?" Costa said, and laughed. "Don't tell me you believe in ghosts and the like?"

"Only fools don't. We are not alone in this world. There are presences older than our kind, and shades are abroad in the witching hour."

"What drivel!" Costa chortled, and they walked out of hearing.

134

They were amateurs, these bounty killers, Nate grimly reflected. As green as grass at woodcraft. Infants who chattered when they should be silent and did not know enough to cover each other's backs as they wound among the boles.

Rising, Nate padded after them. He could not pass up an opportunity to whittle the odds.

"Anything yet?" hollered a searcher.

"If we'd found him, don't you think you'd know it?" Costa responded.

Amateurs, Nate reiterated, flowing as silently as the shades Sprague had alluded to.

Up ahead was the clearing, and the cabin.

From out of a cluster of saplings came a hail. "What in hell is going on?" And into the open strode Bates with Wallace on his heels.

"What is all the ruckus about?"

"King has escaped," Sprague informed them, "and if we don't find him, Jigger will throw a fit."

"He'll try to reach his family, I'll warrant," Bates guessed. "Wallace, you keep an eye on the front of his cabin. If he makes a break for the door, shoot him."

"But only to wound him!" Sprague exclaimed. "We need him alive to trade for the boss, remember?"

Hunkered behind a pine, Nate debated how best to get inside intact. The front door was out of the question, but there was always the window. He had come out through it; he could go in the same way. All he had to do was sneak past the bounty men.

First, though, Nate sank onto all fours and snuck

toward a figure fifteen feet away. In the pale starlight he recognized Evans. A muscular gent, Evans was armed with a brace of pistols, a rifle, and not one but two Bowies, one of which was Nate's.

Nate came within pouncing range and coiled to spring. He must strike swiftly. A couple of smashing blows to the throat should suffice, and then he would grab the weapons and bolt for the cabin. He would fire a shot or two as he ran, and trust in the general confusion to make it to the cabin window and dive inside.

Nate was unfurling when a sharp *click* warned him someone had come up on him undetected from the rear, a commendable feat for a city dweller.

"Don't move. I'd rather not shoot you, but I will if you give me cause."

"Jigger," Nate said.

"None other. I was hoping the others would keep you occupied."

Nate had been duped. The whole time he had been eluding the others, Jigger had been stalking him. "What now?"

"What else? Hold your hands out where I can see them and do exactly as I say, and you get to live."

"And if I don't?" Nate challenged.

"I need you alive, but there's no reason I can't put a slug in your leg. It won't interfere with the swap. So go right ahead and try something."

By now some of the others were converging with their guns leveled.

"You caught him!" Sprague declared.

"I sure couldn't rely on you to do it, could I?"

was Jigger's acidic reply. "It's a wonder any of you can dress yourselves without help."

"We're not as bad as all that," Evans said.

"That's right," Costa agreed. "And we're mighty tired of your never-ending insults."

"Says you," Jigger declared. "But I'll hold my tongue if two of you misfits will take hold of Nate King and bring him back to camp. His company has been sorely missed." At that, Jigger laughed.

To be so close and then be caught rankled Nate. He had brought it on himself by being careless, which only made it worse.

"No tricks, you hear?" Evans seized his left forearm. "Why take a bullet when you don't have to, eh?"

Another killer appeared, one whose name Nate did not know, a lanky man in ill-fitting clothes who favored a wide-brimmed hat in the Spanish style. He grabbed Nate's other arm.

"Careful does it, boys," Jigger said. "He's half heathen, this one, and capable of anything."

"I'm no heathen," Nate said indignantly.

"Oh no? You're married to a Shoshone squaw, aren't you? Rumor has it her tribe adopted you, too. That makes you half heathen in my book."

Covered and surrounded, Nate had to meekly submit to being led back to the fire. But how he yearned to get his hands on a weapon and lay about him with abandon! "A lot of so-called heathens are better people than some whites I've met." Nate glared pointedly at Jigger, who, surprisingly, laughed.

"Nice try, but you can't get my goat that easy. I've been called worse by sots who had cussin' down to an art."

"To think," Nate said, changing the subject, "you came all this way to die."

Jigger was unruffled. "No. I came all this way for my share of the ten thousand dollars on your head. Which, thanks to you killing some of us off, now stands at over a thousand dollars for each of us. That's more than most folks earn in two or three years of scraping by."

"The more of you die, the bigger your shares?"

"That's how we worked it out," Jigger confirmed. "It's fairest for everyone. All we have to do to collect is stay alive."

"Do the others know you aim to kill them before you reach civilization?" Nate casually inquired.

Jigger stopped short and slowly said, "I would never do a thing like that, and they know it."

"Sure you wouldn't," Nate said, delighted by the suspicious looks bestowed on the second-in-command by the others. A seed had been planted.

"You think you're clever, but you're not," Jigger said, his countenance as frigid as a North Sea iceberg. "If I really wanted it all to myself, I wouldn't be working so hard to save Lucian Traggard."

"If you were the only one alive, I wonder if you would try so hard?" Nate said with an emphasis none of his listeners were likely to miss.

Jigger whirled, a long-bladed knife in his hand. "Keep a rein on that mouth of yours, mountain man, or when we do the swap, you'll be minus your tongue."

Sprague, as usual, was not shy about speaking his mind. "Why would he say a thing like that? About you killing us, I mean?"

"Any idiot can see he's trying to turn us against each other," Jigger said. "Pay him no heed."

The cutthroats ringing Nate exchanged looks that did not bode well for their temporary leader.

Jigger was in a foul mood when they reached the fire. He commanded Nate to sit and had Evans bind his wrists in front of him where they could be seen at all times. Jigger did not order his ankles bound. Instead, he positioned Sprague and Costa on each side of Nate with their cocked rifles pointed at his chest.

"I'd like to see you get away now."

"But this means we'll have to stay up all night," Sprague complained.

"You'll be relieved in a couple of hours so you can sleep," Jigger promised. Then, bending so his face was inches from Nate's right ear, he whispered, "You made a bad mistake back there, mister. If it's the last thing I do, I'm going to make you suffer. Mark my words."

Nate had been threatened so many times that one more was of no consequence, except that Jigger glared at him for over an hour, until he curled up on his side. Even then, Jigger continued to glare until he closed his eyes and feigned sleep, a testament to the depth of the small man's hatred.

Slumber did not come right away. Nate rolled and tossed. He was worried about Winona. Worried she would show up and ride right into the guns of the bounty killers. He must prevent that from happening by any and every means he could think of.

In due course, Nate's overwrought nerves and battered body succumbed. He slept as one dead, without dreaming or stirring, oblivious to everything around him until a sharp pang roused him from a black emptiness to return to the world of the living. When he did not open his eyes right away, he received another kick to the ribs.

"Wake up, damn you."

Nate opened his eyes as a foot swept at his body. Without thinking, even though bound, he caught hold of the leg with both hands. Instantly, a pistol muzzle was shoved in his face.

"I'd let go were I you," Wallace growled.

Nate looked up into brown mirrors of pure spite. "I'm awake," he said, letting go and sitting up.

A pink band framed the eastern horizon. Dawn would break soon, but for a little while yet stars speckled the firmament, sparkling like so many diamonds on a backdrop of blueberry-colored cloth.

Nate could not help thinking that Winona might be staring at those exact same stars. He prayed she had not come after him. He prayed she was safe with his son and daughter. But she was not the kind to sit idle when the man she loved might be in trouble. She was strong-willed, his wife. When she needed to do something she did it, and woe to anyone or anything that stood in her way.

Decades ago, when they met, Nate had not fully appreciated exactly how strong she was. But then, he had not appreciated a lot of her traits. In the rosy flush of fledgling love, he had seen her as he wanted to see her and not as she truly was. A common enough failing, if it could be called that.

When couples were young and in love, their love eclipsed all else. Special traits were lost in the blinding glow of emotions run rampant. Only later, with the distance of time and the cooling of ardor, did lovers see each other as they really and truly were. For some that was a shock. For others, it made no difference, since they still loved the other person as dearly as ever, if not more so.

Therein lay one of life's mysteries. How two people grew more in love with the passing of years. How the more deeply they came to know one another, the more deeply they cared.

Love was like a glue that cemented two people together for all time, provided the glue was not neglected, that it was not allowed to dry and chip and wither until none was left.

A rifle muzzle jabbed Nate hard in the spine, ending his reverie. "Don't do that again," Nate said.

"Or what?" Sprague asked. "You'll take my rifle away from me and beat me over the head with it?" He tittered merrily. "If you don't want to be poked, then do as you're told."

"I didn't hear you say anything," Nate said.

"Are your ears plugged with wax? It wasn't me. It was him." Sprague nodded at Jigger.

"It will be a bit yet before it's light enough for

the swap. In the meantime, you have the honor of burying Ira Stimms."

A gray pallor lent the dead man the aspect of a spectral effigy. His eyes were closed, one hand pressed to the throat he had clawed at as he gasped his last breath.

"Get cracking," Jigger said.

Bates and Costa accompanied him.

Nate was handed a small shovel from off one of the horses the bounty men had recovered. With Stimms across his shoulders, Nate was prodded at gunpoint into the trees.

"Any spot you like," Bates informed him. "It doesn't make any difference to us, and it sure as hell doesn't make any difference to Ira."

"Dead is dead," Costa said. "The maggots eat you, and that's the end of it."

"You don't believe in a hereafter?" Bates asked. "In heaven and hell and angels and demons?"

"Posh and fairy tales. There's no life after we shed this one. Ashes to ashes, dust to dust, and that's all." Bates poked Nate with his rifle. "How about you, mountain man? What do you believe?"

Nate had gone so far into the woods that the rest of the bounty men were no longer in view. Stopping, he hooked his left elbow around one of the dead man's legs. "I believe some people are more stupid than others," he said, and swung the body down and around. At the right instant, he let go and Ira Stimms smashed into Costa, bearing him to earth.

Bates squawked in surprise and brought his rifle

up, but he was much too slow. Nate slammed the shovel against Bates's jaw with a loud *spang*. Bates staggered but did not collapse, and Nate swung again, striking him on the side of the head. Bates folded like an accordion.

Costa, meanwhile, with Stimms's body across his legs, was frantically trying to get his hands on the rifle he had dropped. "You're going to bleed, King! Do you hear me? You're going to damn well bleed for this!"

"One of us is," Nate said, and brought the shovel down on the crown of Costa's head. Costa pitched to the grass, groaned once, and was still.

Smiling, Nate threw the shovel aside and reached to claim the rifle for himself. Suddenly, a pistol blasted and a miniature dirt geyser erupted under his fingers.

Jigger and Sprague were charging toward him, Jigger holding two pistols, one with smoke curling from the barrel. He took aim with the other.

Flinging himself into the undergrowth, Nate heard the pistol go off. There was no pain, no jolt of impact. Jigger had missed. Winding and weaving like a madman, Nate raced as fast as he could fly toward the clearing. Another gun cracked; the slug smacked into a fir next to him. Someone shouted, but he could not make out what they were saying.

Almost too late, Nate remembered that two bounty men were posted near the cabin. Bates and Wallace had been relieved by Evans and someone else. He looked up and there they were, rising from concealment with their rifles wedged to their shoulders. Veering to the south, Nate winced when a slug cored a tree trunk and sent stinging slivers into his cheek and neck.

The sleep had done wonders. As sore as he was, as badly bruised and hurting, the short rest had invigorated him. Nate bubbled with vitality, where before he had little to spare. Twenty yards he ran, then thirty, and his legs did not tire and his lungs did not give out.

One thing about living in the crucible men called the Rockies—it honed a man like a whetstone honed a knife. She was a harsh mistress, the wilderness, and she exacted a toll on those who endured her varied and many hardships. Human sinew became as iron, human reflexes as that of the mountain lion and the lynx. Survival was a cauldron in which thews were forged to resemble molten steel. Taxed to its utmost day after day, the human body melted away its fat and flab like a hot candle melted its own wax.

Thus it was that Nate King soon outdistanced those after him. None had close to his fleetness of limb.

When the sounds of pursuit faded, Nate changed direction. To the northwest lay the cabin, his aim to reach it before sunrise and slip inside.

Harsh shouts warned of searchers to his right, so Nate angled to his left. He would be damned if he would let them snare him a third time.

"He went this way!"

"No he didn't! He's over here somewhere!"

Soon Nate spied the corral and bore to the west

to come up on the cabin from the rear. He was watching over a shoulder, convinced as he was that the bounty men were all to the east of him. Which made his bewilderment all the greater when without warning a figure loomed directly in his path and a rifle barrel gleamed in the rapidly increasing light of the impending dawn.

Chapter Ten

Nate King had been worried about his wife. Worried Winona would show up looking for him and become embroiled in the conflict that threatened to take his life and might well take hers. He had worried the whole night long and every waking moment since he was roused from slumber by a sharp kick in the side.

But now who should Nate see when he stopped to confront the figure that had appeared in front of him brandishing a rifle? "Evelyn?" Nate blurted in stunned amazement. "What in the world are you doing here?"

Out of the brush stepped Chases Rabbits, beaming happily. "Me bring her, Grizzly Killer!" he declared. "We come find you! Do good, yes?"

Nate could have punched him. As it was, he grabbed each of them by an arm and propelled them deeper into the trees and yanked them down onto their knees. "Hush, you infant!" he whispered. "We're in great danger. There are men out to kill me, and now they'll try to kill you, too."

"What men?" Chases Rabbits loudly asked, laying hold of the bow slung across his chest.

"Quiet!" Nate shushed him by clamping a hand to the young warrior's mouth. "Can't you hear that?"

Feet hammered the ground and the underbrush rustled to the passage of nearby searchers.

Nate removed his hand and turned to Evelyn, who had the presence of mind to stay silent. Embracing her, he whispered, "Where is your mother? Why didn't she come?"

"She's probably on her way," Evelyn whispered. "Chases Rabbits and I took a couple of horses while the rest were butchering the buffalo and came on ahead to find you." She met his gaze unflinchingly. "It was my mount that ran off. I was the one who had to come."

"I wish you hadn't," Nate said, and let it go at that. Scolding her would not change the plight they were in.

"What's going on, Pa? Where are the Stuarts?"

Briefly, Nate explained, ending with "Where did you leave your mounts?"

"About a hundred yards back," Evelyn whispered, pointing. "We heard shooting and came on foot to see what it was about."

"That was smart," Nate said. "Now I want you to turn around, get on those horses, and ride like

147

the wind. Tell Shakespeare and Zach what I'm up against. If they ride hard, they can be here by midnight."

"What about the rest of us?"

"Someone has to watch over our belongings and the horses." Nate thought that was the end of it and pecked her on the cheek. "Off you go, Daughter."

"No."

"How's that again?"

"I'm staying with you, Pa," Evelyn whispered. "And nothing you can say will change my mind. I'm a King, and Kings stick up for one another. Isn't that what you've always told us?"

"This is no time to argue. I want you safe. That's more important than anything." The rustling in the brush had faded, but Nate knew the bounty men had not given up.

"The important thing is helping you stay alive," Evelyn asserted. "You don't even have a gun. Here." She offered him her rifle.

Although Nate was deeply touched, he pushed the Hawken toward her. "Keep it. Do as I've told you. Please. I have to get to the Stuarts while I still can."

"I won't go. Be mad if you have to, but I love you too much to desert you when you need me the most."

A warm feeling grew deep in Nate and spread through his entire being. His throat constricted and he had to cough to whisper, "You're as pigheaded as your mother. If you were younger, I would spank you."

"I doubt that," Evelyn whispered. "You never

once laid a hand on me all the years I was growing up."

That was more Winona's doing than Nate's. Shoshones did not believe in physically punishing their children. They felt it did as much harm, if not more, than whatever deed the children were being punished for. Instead of spanking them, or taking a switch to their backsides, Shoshone parents made their displeasure known by treating the misbehaved child as an outcast; essentially, they would not talk to the offender or do things for the child they would normally do. It shamed their children into behaving, and as Nate could personally attest, it was remarkably effective.

"Me not go either," Chases Rabbits whispered, thumping his skinny chest. "Me help Grizzly Killer rub out bad whites."

"Someone needs to ride for help."

"Me not leave Blue Flower," Chases Rabbits stubbornly refused. "Me pig with head, too."

A twig snapped, and Nate placed his hands on their shoulders and practically pushed them face-first into the ground. Lying flat, he saw scuffed black boots move stealthily through the woods a score of feet to the east.

"Any sign of him?" came a holler from farther away. From Jigger.

"Not over here!" replied the owner of the boots; it was Sprague.

"Keep looking! That bastard has to be around here somewhere! We're almost ready, and we don't want him interfering!"

Nate watched the black boots wind northward, all the while wondering what Jigger meant by "almost ready." Almost ready for what? He had foiled their scheme to swap him for Traggard. What could they be up to now? The answer hit him with the force of a physical blow. "Stay here," he whispered to Evelyn and her suitor, "and I mean *stay here*." Then he was up and racing for the cabin, and if he made too much noise, so be it.

Jigger was not wasting any time. The sun was starting to rise. A golden crescent crowned the horizon, and the woods were twice as bright as they had been mere minutes before.

Nate saw the corral, and beyond, crouched at the base of the south wall, Bates and Wallace had jammed a keg of powder into the hole and were inserting a strip of cloth as a fuse. Nate didn't know if it was the same keg or another, but that was irrelevant. In a few seconds, they would light the fuse and run. He must not let that happen or the Stuarts were doomed.

Suddenly, there was a harsh yell and the boom of a rifle, but Sprague missed. Then Nate was at the corral and vaulted over the top rail without breaking stride.

Wallace spun and rose, clawing for the pistols at his waist. Bates had a fire steel and flint out and was bent over the keg.

Lowering a shoulder, Nate slammed into Wallace like a mad bull. The impact sent Wallace stumbling back against the cabin. Turning, Nate sprang at Bates, but the worst had come to pass: The fuse was already lit. Bates leaped back, grinning wolfishly, and shouted, "Run, Wallace! Run! She's going to blow!"

The bounty men fled as Nate dived at the keg. He grasped the fuse, singeing his fingertips, and had to let go. Wrenching the keg from the hole, he whirled and ran to the rails and hurled the keg with all his strength.

"Pa?"

Time seemed to stop. There was Nate, half across the top rail. There was the keg, high in the air and arcing downward. And there was Evelyn, almost directly under it. Once again she had not listened. She had followed him.

Pure horror flooded through Nate. Horror so potent, he was paralyzed. He could not move, could not shout the warning that his brain screamed at him to shout. He envisioned the explosion, envisioned his daughter being blown into a thousand fragments.

"Pa?" Evelyn called out again, hurrying toward him. "Are you all right?"

"Noooooooooo!" Nate found his voice and gripped the top rail to swing over it. He saw Evelyn stop in confusion, saw a buckskin-clad stripling hurtle out of nowhere and fling himself at her, and then thunder that was not thunder seemed to shake the very sky and the earth under Nate's feet, and an invisible wall slammed into him, lifting him and catapulting him as if he were a leaf caught in a gale. Somersaulting end over end, he tumbled almost to the cabin and lay dazed, his ears ringing.

Fear for Evelyn spurred Nate into rising and shaking himself to clear his head. Astoundingly, he was unscathed except for more bruises. In the aftermath of the blast, the world seemed unnaturally quiet.

His legs wobbly, Nate crossed the corral. The rails he had been leaning on were splintered and one of the uprights had been uprooted and shattered. Shouts intruded on the ringing in his ears, but they were strangely muffled. Stepping over the destroyed fence, he took a few steps, then stopped, his heart in his mouth.

A hole had been blasted out of the vegetation. Trees and brush and even grass had been torn asunder or else flattened as if by a whirlwind of titanic proportions, leaving a circle some forty feet in circumference. In the center of that circle were two prone forms.

"God, no," Nate breathed, and barely heard himself speak. The blast had done something to his hearing.

Frantic, Nate dashed to the crumpled bodies and sank to his knees. Chases Rabbits was on top of Evelyn. The young Crow had pushed her down and protected her with his own body. Both ears were bleeding and red rivulets trickled from the Crow's nose. In addition, a slender spike of wood from a pine tree had embedded itself in his right shoulder.

Exercising extreme care, Nate slid the youth off Evelyn. She was on her stomach, one arm flung out, the other bent under her. Her ears were bleeding, too, although not as badly. Like Chases Rabbits, her clothes were covered with dirt and bits of greenery and slivers. Shimmering dust motes swarmed in the air about them.

"Please," Nate said, and put a finger to her neck. His joy at finding a pulse was boundless. He did the same with Chases Rabbits. They were both alive, but there was no telling how much internal damage they had suffered.

Nate started to gently roll Evelyn over and had to stop when a wave of nausea nearly blacked him out. He felt fit to retch. The world spun, and he placed both hands to his temples until the sensation passed.

It was best not to move them, but Nate did not have that luxury. Scooping Evelyn into his arms, he shifted to stand and carry her to the cabin. Mocking laughter rooted him on his knees.

"Well, well, well. Look at what we have here, boys."

The remark came to Nate as if from the far end of a long tunnel. He blinked up into the sadistic countenance of the man called Jigger. Others ringed him: Sprague, Costa, Bates, Wallace, Evans, all of them, smirking and grinning and eyeing him like a pack of ravenous wolves eyeing a bull elk they were about to attack.

"That girl must be his brat," Jigger said. "And the Injun must be Shoshone kin of theirs."

Nate coiled to spring. With Evelyn in his arms there was not much he could do other than make a break for the front of the cabin and hope he made it inside without being shot to ribbons.

"So now we have two of the four we need to collect the ten-thousand-dollar bounty," Bates said.

"Let's kill them and be done with it," Wallace urged.

"Have you forgotten Traggard?" Jigger responded. "He's the only one who can arrange for us to be paid." Jigger shook his head. "No, we go through with the swap. Only now we keep the girl and the redskin."

"Can't we slit the Injun's throat, at least?" Sprague asked.

"What if there are more hereabouts?" Jigger rejoined. "They won't try anything so long as we have one of their own."

"You hope," Sprague said.

Their words were louder and clearer; Nate's hearing was returning. He noticed the ringing in his ears was almost gone, but now both his ears hurt like the blazes.

"On your feet, mountain man," Jigger directed. "Evans, you and Wallace tote the redskin."

"Why us?" Evans asked.

"Because I said so." Jigger nudged Nate with a toe. "Didn't you hear me? Carry your brat to the lake and be quick about it."

Nate glanced at the cabin. He thought it peculiar the Stuarts had not ventured out to investigate the explosion. For that matter, there had been no sign of them since the day before.

"I wouldn't take forever," Jigger advised. "Not unless you want one of us to carry her for you."

Nate rarely indulged in threats, but he indulged in one now. "I'll kill the man who touches her."

"Then on your feet, damn it, and do as I say. We don't have all day."

The weakness in Nate's legs had faded. Clasping Evelyn to his chest, he painfully rose.

Several of the bounty killers closed in, and Bates said, "Nice and slow, if you don't mind."

As if Nate would further endanger Evelyn. She was breathing, yes, but she was so pale and so still that he dreaded she might be bleeding internally. Severe hemorrhaging, as the doctors called it, was nearly always fatal.

As they passed the front of the cabin, Nate glanced at the window and the door but saw no one peering out. There was no sign of life whatsoever. It puzzled him, but he was too upset about Evelyn to give it any thought.

"This Injun smells funny," Wallace commented, one arm around Chases Rabbits. He sniffed a few times. "God Almighty. What in hell does this buck use in his hair, anyhow?"

"Bear fat," Nate absently answered.

"No wonder he stinks," Evans said. "Who in their right mind uses renderings when axle grease slicks just as well?"

Nate did not bother to point out that since Indians did not own prairie schooners or buckboards, they had no need for axle grease. Which, come to think of it, was not any more fragrant than bear fat.

"Injuns sure do stupid things," Wallace said.

"Like wearin' feathers in their hair and livin' in te-pees made of buffalo hides instead of real houses."

"They're red gnats, is what they are," Sprague declared. "Andy Jackson had it right. The only good redskin is a dead redskin."

In single file they proceeded down the trail to the lakeshore and over to the fire, which was almost out. Nate carefully laid Evelyn on a blanket. Chases Rabbits was unceremoniously dumped beside her, and groaned.

The bounty men stood back, watching him, and Sprague asked, "What do we do now, Jigger?"

Before the little man could answer, a voice with a Southern drawl rose from out of the trees. "Drop your guns and throw your arms in the air!"

A tingle of excitement coursed through Nate. The Stuarts had snuck from the cabin while the killers were occupied with him, and now had the advantage.

Jigger and the rest spun, but they did not hike their hands; they leveled their guns. Jigger, ever the craftiest, took a quick step and touched the muzzle of his rifle to Nate's head. "Take a shot at us and I swear your friend here dies! Him and his girl!"

Robert Stuart barely hesitated. "Then how about a trade? Your man for Nate King and those other two?"

"You took the words right out of my mouth, mister," Jigger answer. "We'll swap King for Lucian Traggard. But only King. We keep the girl and the Injun."

Nate tried to spot the South Carolinians in the

trees, but they were too well concealed. He did glimpse something else: a four-legged shape poised low to the ground, its fangs bared.

"Traggard for all three," Robert Stuart hollered.

"Three for one ain't hardly fair," Jigger angrily responded. "It's Nate King and only Nate King!"

"That's unacceptable," Robert yelled. He was quiet for half a minute. "Need I point out you're in the open and we're not? We do it my way, river rat, and I give you my word we will retire to the cabin without firin' a shot."

"Damned decent of you," Jigger said, "but need *I* point out that we can kill all three before we go down? Seems to me we have you over a barrel."

Robert Stuart did not reply. Jigger snickered at Nate and said, "Who is that, anyhow? A friend of yours? With that accent, he's sure not your 'breed son."

"My son was never here," Nate said. "None of my family were." His deep emotional shock at Evelyn's near-death was giving way to a burning resentment at those responsible.

"Oh really?" Jigger said. "And what's she?" He pointed at Evelyn. "Don't treat me like a jackass and I won't treat you like one. Your wife and son are in those trees with your friends. I know it and you know it."

"What I know," Nate said grimly, "is that I have seldom wanted to bury anyone as much as I want to bury you."

Jigger laughed, but the mirth was not reflected by his eyes. Jabbing his rifle against Nate's cheek, he growled, "That's mutual, mountain man. You've given us a heap of trouble. Four dead, and Traggard held prisoner. But now the tables have turned." He shifted toward the woods and raised his voice. "Do you hear me in there? Release Lucian Traggard within the next sixty seconds or I'll splatter Nate King's brains all over creation."

"I have a better idea!" Robert Stuart shouted.

"What would that be?" was Jigger's guarded reply.

Nate and the bounty killers all heard the command. Sharp and clear it rang out: *"Sic 'em!"*

From out of the trees streaked four canine furies.

"The dogs!" Sprague bawled. "Dear God, it's the dogs!"

Fur-clad quicksilver, the four hounds flowed over the ground as if in defiance of gravity. They were so incredibly quick that only one man was able to snap off a shot before the hounds reached them. That one man was Jigger, and in his haste, he missed.

Then the hounds were in among the bounty killers, leaping and biting and snarling. Bedlam ensued. Evans went down, screeching and thrashing, a hound clamped to his throat. Another dog had its fangs buried in Bates's arm and Bates was frantically trying to shake it off. Costa drew a pistol and fired, but the hound he shot at swerved and the heavy ball intended for the dog nicked Sprague in the thigh, and it was Sprague who pitched forward with a shriek of anguish.

Jigger palmed one of his pistols and sought to fix a

bead, but in the mad melee it was impossible. None of the dogs stayed still for more than a heartbeat.

Another scream rang out. As it died, Nate was up and running toward the woods, Evelyn in his arms. At any second, a slug might rip through his back. He saw a figure amid the trees. It was Emory Stuart, beckoning urgently for him to go faster. But he was going as fast as he could.

A hound yipped. Men swore lustily. Pistols cracked. A rifle boomed. Nate reached the woods and hurtled into a thicket, plowing through it like an insane bull, his arms protectively around Evelyn to ward off the branches and barbs. Then Emory was in front of him, clapping him on the shoulder and saying, "You're safe now! But get down!"

Yes, Nate was momentarily out of harm's path, and Evelyn, too, but he laid his daughter at the Southerner's feet, cried out, "Watch over her!" and wheeled and plunged back toward the bedlam.

Chases Rabbits still lay by the fire.

Part of Nate railed at his insanity. He hardly knew the boy. Chases Rabbits was not a member of his family. The Crow did not even belong to the same tribe. But all Nate could think of was how Chases Rabbits had thrown himself on top of Evelyn to shield her from the keg of powder. Nate owed it to the young warrior to do what he could to save him.

Unexpectedly, a piercing whistle from Robert Stuart brought the superbly trained hounds back on the fly. One was limping, another with a hole in its side from which blood sprayed in a fine mist. In their wake they left two of Traggard's men on the ground, one as still as a log, the other clutching a ravaged throat and rolling back and forth and blubbering hysterically.

A couple of shots were sent after the dogs but missed. Most of the killers were hastily reloading.

Jigger had already done so and was the only one to perceive what would happen next. "Get down!" he bawled, and threw himself flat.

"Now!" Robert Stuart shouted. "Do it *now*!"

A ragged volley pealed to the clouds. All five of the Stuarts had fired, Arvil shooting from the hip because of the bullet hole in his bandaged shoulder.

A split second before, Nate threw himself flat in order not to be accidentally struck.

Most of the bounty men were caught flat-footed, but not all. Jigger dived for the earth. So did Sprague. Those still on their feet were blown off them. Wallace was shot through the head. Bates was hit twice, in the chest and the jaw, the heavy-caliber slug ripping half his jawbone from his face.

Nate whooped for joy. His elation, though, was premature.

Jigger and Sprague were up and running toward the horses. In a remarkable display of agility, Jigger seized hold of a saddle, swung lithely up, and spurred the horse into motion. Sprague was ungainly by comparison but made it onto a horse and sped after Jigger toward the forest to the north.

"Don't let them get away!" Robert Stuart shouted, and flew from cover to send a pistol ball after them.

Arvil and Jethro and Lee and Emory imitated his example, but only Jethro and Emory fired, and neither appeared to score.

"We did it!" Arvil whooped. "We drove them off!"

In their excitement the Stuarts had not noticed Evans. His throat horribly torn, bleeding a torrent, Evans fumbled for a flintlock.

Nate yelled a warning, but the Southerners were yipping so loudly, they didn't hear him.

Evans did not take aim. He was too weak and fading fast. He simply pointed the pistol and fired.

Jethro Stuart was laughing in glee. The slug went into his open mouth and burst out the rear of his skull, coring his cranium and his brain. He died without ever knowing who shot him.

Instantly, the remaining Stuarts spun on Evans, who was on his elbows, gasping for air like a fish out of water. Since their guns were expended, the Stuarts rushed him with drawn knives and hatchets. It was over in a span of seconds, as ghastly a display as Nate ever witnessed of chopping a human being into bits. Lee, in particular, kept swinging his hatchet again and again and again.

Nate ran to Chases Rabbits and rolled the young Crow over. He was still alive, thank God, but he was still bleeding from his ears and his nose.

A shadow fell across them, and Nate looked up. "I can't thank you enough, you and your kin. I'm sorry for your loss."

"It's not done," Robert said. "Two got away, and there's Traggard." He jabbed a thumb at Emory and Lee. "Fetch the miserable vermin who brought this down on our heads." As they jogged into the pines, Robert turned back to Nate. "I know you told us to stay in the cabin, but I couldn't take being cooped up any longer. So I laid a trap for these polecats."

"And I'm glad you did," Nate said sincerely. "You did fine."

Robert stared at Jethro. "Not fine enough."

Nate was lifting Chases Rabbits by the shoulders to sit him up when Emory and Lee flew out of the woods as if the trees were ablaze.

"It's Traggard!" Lee declared. "He's not where we left him! He's escaped!" Lee swung toward Nate. "That's not all! He took your daughter with him!"

Chapter Eleven

Tracks told the story. While the Stuarts battled the bounty men, Lucian Traggard had freed himself by rubbing his wrists against a jagged boulder until he severed the whangs that bound him. Then he had headed north, and as fickle fate would have it, he had stumbled on Evelyn where Nate left her, unconscious and unprotected.

Nate felt sick. He wanted to roar with rage. He wanted to flail about him with a tomahawk or a club. He wanted to shoot something. But it would not do to lose his self-control. To save the daughter he loved so dearly, he must stay calm and go about it efficiently and rationally.

"We're awful sorry, Nate," Robert Stuart apologized for the twentieth time. "I never figured he could slip away that fast."

"It's my fault," Nate said. "I left her and I shouldn't have." Guilt weighed on him like the weight of the world on Atlas's shoulders. The only bright spot was that he had reclaimed his weapons; he now had his Hawken, both pistols, his Bowie, and the tomahawk. "I'm going after her."

"Not alone you're not."

"Someone has to watch over Chases Rabbits," Nate said. The young Crow was still out. They had tried to revive him by cutting a strip from a blanket, dipping it in the lake, and applying the soaked strip to his brow and face, but all Chases Rabbits did was groan. At least the bleeding had stopped.

"It doesn't take all of us to look after one person," Robert responded. "Lee and Arvil will tote him to the cabin. Emory and me will go with you."

Nate surprised himself by hesitating. Evelyn was his daughter; he should save her himself. And, too, the bounty killers were after him, not the Stuarts. But with Evelyn's life in the balance, he could ill afford false pride. "There's only one horse." The rest belonging to Traggard's party had been spooked by the gunfire. "You'll have to come after me on foot." Nate did not have the time to spare to fetch his bay or the mounts Evelyn and Chases Rabbits had ridden.

"Don't you worry about us," Robert assured him. "We've been trackin' since we were knee-high to calves. The trail will be easy to follow."

Swinging onto the roan, Nate paused. "If something should happen to me, I'd be obliged if you saw it through and returned my daughter safe and sound to my wife."

Robert Stuart nodded. "Count on it."

Nate jabbed his heels. The killers had a fifteen-minute head start, but he would whittle that down soon enough. He rode at a reckless rate, his insides churning. If anything happened to Evelyn, he would never forgive himself. The thought stabbed acute fear through his entire being. "Please let her be all right," he prayed aloud.

The hoofprints of Jigger's and Sprague's mounts were plain enough, but they were not who Nate was after. He found where Traggard, carrying Evelyn, paralleled their tracks, and Nate proceeded to follow Traggard's. Since Traggard was on foot, by holding to a trot Nate rapidly narrowed the gap.

Less than half a mile from the lake, Nate came over a low rise and reined up in consternation on beholding a figure on the ground seventy-five feet away. Recognition hit, and he was about to fly to her side when his common sense took over. Instead, he reined to the right into thick vegetation and dismounted.

Evelyn was being used as bait. Traggard was out there somewhere, waiting for Nate to come rushing up. Nate did not know if Traggard had gotten hold of a gun, but he would act on the assumption Traggard had. Wrapping the roan's reins around a low tree limb, he advanced cautiously on foot.

It was a nightmare, that stalk. Not because Traggard was waiting for a chance to strike, but because Nate could not stand to see Evelyn lying there, hurt and vulnerable and helpless. Every fatherly instinct he had compelled him to fly to her, but that was exactly the mistake Traggard counted on him making.

It took all the willpower Nate possessed to do it right. To go slowly, to stick to cover and place each moccasin down as if he were treading on broken glass. Every few steps, he stopped to scan the woods and listen. A simple precaution that could mean the difference between surviving and dying.

All went well until Nate was five or six yards from his daughter. Then Evelyn unexpectedly twitched and stirred and rose sluggishly onto her elbows, saying in the little-girl tone she so seldom used anymore, "Pa? Where are you?"

The sight, and her need, were more than Nate could bear. Breaking from cover, he sped to her side and fell to a knee next to her, saying, "I'm here. Don't worry, princess."

Evelyn sank back down. "I feel awful," she said woozily. "What happened? The last thing I remember is Chases Rabbits yelling something, and then the loudest noise I've ever heard."

Nate tore his eyes away to scour the brush. Any moment now, Lucian Traggard was likely to pounce.

"Where is he?" Evelyn asked. "And where am I? I don't see the cabin anywhere."

"Lie still," Nate said, twisting to check behind him. "I'll explain in a bit." He was pleased she did not press him, but then, his tone and his manner were enough to alert her they were in peril. *Where is he?* he wondered, half wishing Traggard would get it over with. But nothing happened. Bathed in the warm glow of sunlight, the forest was a portrait of tranquillity.

The seconds dragged by, and just when the tension was at its peak, hoofs pounded to the south. Nate straightened, jerking the Hawken to his shoulder, but he did not have a clear shot.

Lucian Traggard was on the roan. Bent low over its neck, Traggard lashed it with the reins and flung a taunting grin at Nate.

Little did he realize that Nate was happy to see him go. "All he wanted was the horse," Nate said in profound relief.

Within moments, the fleeing killer was out of sight. Nate waited another minute to be sure, then squatted and lifted Evelyn in his arms and bent his steps toward the cabin.

"What are you doing?" Evelyn weakly asked. "I'm not helpless. I can walk."

"Hush. You need rest and lots of it." Nate detailed all that had occurred since the keg exploded, and she listened in attentive silence, interrupting only once to ask, "How bad is Chases Rabbits?"

"Bad" was all Nate would say.

"All the times I've teased him," Evelyn said, "and he goes and throws himself on top of me to save me."

"You shouldn't talk. You should rest."

"I've never taken him seriously," Evelyn said. "It's made me laugh to think he wants me for his wife. It's too silly for words. Then he goes and does something like this."

"Didn't you hear me say to hush up?"

"He really must care for me, Pa. And I've treated him like a simpleton. I hope he lives so I can say I'm sorry."

"What's important to me is that *you* live," Nate declared. "How do you feel? Can you hear all right? Is there pain anywhere?"

"I feel sick and my head is throbbing, but I can hear just fine," Evelyn answered. She stifled a yawn. "I feel so darned tired, I could sleep for a week."

"That's normal," Nate said. "Stop talking and try and get some rest now."

Evelyn ignored him. "For someone so goofy, he sure is brave. He reminds me a lot of you."

Nate was vaguely uneasy with the comparison. "I don't see how." He was as different from Chases Rabbits as the sun from the moon. The more he considered it, the more it led him to the conclusion. "We don't have a thing in common." He pecked her on the forehead. "Now, will you *please* stop talking."

"I almost died, didn't I?"

"You came as close as anyone ever wants this side of the grave," Nate acknowledged, and repressed a shudder at exactly how close it had been.

"I've always said the wilderness was a dangerous place to live," Evelyn quietly remarked.

"I know, I know," Nate said. She had harped on it for years. It was her main reason for wanting to leave the Rockies. "But you can't blame the wilderness this time. Traggard and his men are from east of the Mississippi. They were born and bred in civilization, where everyone is nice and kind and never hurts anyone else."

"Could you be any more sarcastic?"

Nate had to remind himself that his youngest

was growing up. She was no longer his "little girl." In some respects she was more mature than Zach. "Sorry. But I'm sick and tired of hearing how wonderful civilization is and how terrible the Rockies are."

"Have you heard me say that once since we came back from our last trip east?" Evelyn asked.

Nate had to think a bit. "No. I can't say as I have. But you'll get around to complaining again sooner or later."

"No, Pa, I won't. I've learned my lesson. Civilization has as many dangers as the mountains. More, even. I learned a lot when I was kidnapped by Athena Borke. I learned there's a dark side to our natures, a side that makes people more dangerous than all the grizzlies and mountain lions ever born."

To say Nate was flabbergasted was an understatement. She had criticized the wilds for so many years, he never, ever expected her attitude to change. "It's nice that you finally see civilization isn't heaven on earth."

"The truth is that people do worse things to themselves than wild beasts ever do," Evelyn went on. "People murder, they maim, they makes slaves of one another. Those with money and power lord it over those without." She stopped, her features downcast. "I heard someone say once life is a bowl of cherries. But it's not. It's a bowl of cherry pits."

"There are a lot of good people, too," Nate said. "There's your family, who love you more than anything. There are people who treat others kindly and never do another soul harm. You can't just look at the dark side."

"I can't ignore it, either." Evelyn rested her cheek on his chest. "It's funny. Until six months ago I always looked at the bright side of things, like Ma and you always told me to do. Now I'm not so sure there really is a bright side."

Deeply troubled, Nate said, "You're too young to be so cynical. We'll talk more about this some other time, after you've recovered."

"Look! Who's that?"

Two men had emerged from the trees and were hastening toward them.

"It's Robert and Emory Stuart. We owe them our lives."

The Southerners were as glad to see Nate as Nate was to see them. With one walking behind him and another walking a few yards ahead, he need not fear an ambush, and said so.

"Ten thousand dollars or not, I doubt those varmints will come back," Robert said. "Not after the lickin' we gave them."

"I hope they do, brother," Emory said. "I'd like to finish the job."

So would Nate. As long as Traggard, Jigger, and Sprague were alive, they were a threat. He was not vengeful by nature. He was not bloodthirsty. But he could not let them get away to return and try to murder his family another day.

Evelyn finally dozed. It had been years since Nate held her for so long, and as much as he hated the circumstances, it touched his heart. She looked so sweet, so pretty, so like an angel. And as daughters went, she seldom gave him cause to scold her. Unlike Zach, who got into hot water every time he turned around.

Robert was thoughtfully staring at her. "I sure do miss my kids. They're a handful, but I can't wait to see them again."

"Do you still intend to transplant your family here?"

"Sure. Why not? But I'll be sure to put up signs sayin' as how the Stuart clan is livin' at the cabin and not the Kings." Robert smiled as he said it.

To Nate, it was like a knife to the gut. It made him realize that disposing of Traggard and the other two was not enough. Not as long as a bounty was being offered through that lawyer in New Orleans.

Smoke was curling from the chimney when they arrived. Arvil had a fire going, and Lee had shot a squirrel and skinned it and put stew on to boil. Chases Rabbits lay on a blanket under the window.

At Robert's direction, more blankets were spread out, and Nate gently deposited Evelyn. As he slid his arm from under her, she opened her eyes and regarded him lovingly.

"Where are we?"

"The cabin. The Stuarts will take care of you. I have something important to do."

"Can't you wait until Zach and Ma get here? They're bound to come once we don't show up."

"By then Traggard will have too much of a lead." Enough that Nate might not overtake him.

Robert Stuart was listening. "It could be we're

171

wrong about him givin' up. He might be out in the woods right this minute, him and those other two, waitin' for a chance to ambush you."

"I'll know soon enough." Nate lightly ran a finger across his daughter's cheek, then went to fetch his bay and the horses Evelyn and Chases Rabbits had ridden. He brought all three to the cabin, filled a water skin and tied it to the bay's saddle, and was ready to depart. He went back inside. "You take care, Daughter," he said, giving her a last hug.

"We'll watch over her like hawks this time," Robert Stuart promised as Nate mounted. Robert gripped the bridle. "Hold on a minute. I have something for you to take along."

Wondering what it could be, Nate was taken aback when Robert came out of the cabin leading Hector. "What's this?"

"He's the best hound I have. Once he has a scent, he never loses it." Robert opened his palm, revealing several of the green whangs used to bind Traggard. "I saved these." He gave them to Nate. "Hector is trained to bring game to bay and hold whatever he's after until I get there. He'll do the same for you."

"Lucian Traggard isn't game."

"Dogs don't know the difference between folks and critters. Besides, I hire out to the county every so often to hunt lawbreakers, and Hector is the best there is at running a man to ground." Robert patted the hound's large head. "All you need are the right commands."

"I'm listening."

Nate committed them to memory, then dubiously

studied the dog. He had never hunted with a hound, and had reservations. "I wouldn't want anything to happen to him."

"He knows about guns, if you'll recollect. To stay shy of them unless he's given the command to sic." Robert Stuart gestured. "Off you go. And good luck."

"Heel, Hector," Nate said, and was impressed when the hound paced the bay, loping at a steady gait. He glanced back once to wave, and Robert responded in kind. Then he concentrated on the task at hand.

First Nate brought Hector to where Traggard had carried Evelyn north from the lake. Dismounting, he held the green whangs under the hound's nose, and after Hector sniffed a few times, he commanded, "Find him, boy! Find him!"

The dog placed its nose close to the ground, gave a loud sniff, and was off like a shot.

Swinging into the saddle, Nate quickly caught up. Robert had said it was important he not let Hector out of his sight. Soon they came to where Traggard had taken the roan. Hector sniffed in circles, evidently fixing on the roan's scent now, and then loped eastward, once again on the trail.

Nate's confidence climbed. He couldn't see how Traggard could shake them unless it rained, and there weren't but three or four puffy clouds in the whole sky. "You're some dog," he said as the hound ate up the miles.

Noon came and went, and still Hector tirelessly stuck to the trail.

It was shortly past one. Nate was nearing the foothills when he found where Traggard had over-taken Jigger and Sprague. Now there were three sets of hoofprints, and three enemies to deal with.

By four it was obvious Nate would not catch them before sunset. He slowed to a walk and gave the hound the command to do the same. Since a campfire might give him away, he made a cold camp and shared his jerky and pemmican with Hector. Later, he crawled under his blanket and pulled the blanket to his chin. No sooner had he done so than a heavy weight pressed against his side. Hector had lain down next to him. He patted the dog's head and Hector placed it on his shoulder.

"If this don't beat all," Nate said, and grinned. But it was not quite so amusing when several times during the night the hound woke him up. Twice because Hector rolled over in his sleep, on top of him. The third time because, much to Nate's astonish-ment, the dog was snoring loud enough to be heard in Missouri.

Dawn arrived crisp and clear. After more pemmi-can, Nate was in the saddle again. The tracks were plain enough that he did not need help, but he had brought the hound this far, so he gave the command to track and off they went.

Tendrils of dust were the first inkling Nate had he was getting close. Half an hour more and he spied three riders lower down among the hills. Reining in among some oaks, Nate stayed put until the trio were lost to sight.

"Careful does it from here on out," Nate said to Hector.

Careful, indeed. A glint of sunlight off metal again drove Nate into hiding. Through his spyglass he saw that Jigger had reined up on the crest of a foothill and was looking back the way they came for any track of pursuit.

"I hope he didn't spot me," Nate said, and realized he was talking to the dog as he would to a person.

Jigger sat on the hilltop a good long while. Either he suspected something or he was being extremely cautious.

Nate climbed down and lounged in the shade. Hector came over and plopped down beside him, and he placed a hand on the dog's great head and scratched behind its ears.

The hound licked his fingers.

Chuckling, Nate rubbed under Hector's chin. "I'm beginning to see why people love dogs so much," he remarked. "My son had a wolf once, but it only let him pet it." He had warned Zach that the wolf might leave one day of its own accord, and sure enough, one winter's day it vanished, never to return. For more than a week, Zach cried himself to sleep every night. It was the last pet the boy ever had.

"Wolves run in packs, but they're not as sociable toward people as dogs are," Nate enlightened Hector. "I sometimes wonder if we adopted that wolf or the wolf adopted us."

Hector yawned, and his long tongue lolled out.

"Will you listen to me?" Nate said in wry humor at his antics. "I jabber more around you than I do around my wife. Why should that be?" He patted Hector's brow and picked up the spyglass.

The hilltop was barren. Jigger had ridden on.

Rising, Nate stepped into the stirrups and resumed the hunt. "By tonight this will be over, one way or another."

Stealth was called for. Nate had to get near them without giving himself away. Fortunately, trees covered many of the slopes. By midafternoon he was a quarter of a mile behind them. They were in good spirits. He saw them talking and laughing. They showed no inclination to go back to the cabin. Maybe they'd had enough and were heading home. If so, it was too little and much too late.

By five they were several thousand feet lower in elevation than they had been at daybreak. Traggard was following a well-worn game trail that would bring them out on the prairie near a creek notable for its swiftly flowing water.

Nate had visited the creek many times. The Shoshones called it Old Woman Creek. Whites had not given it a name yet. Or, to be more precise, the creek had not earned one. Waterways were often named for their discoverer, or for a notable event, as in the case of a river named after a trapper who had been scalped by the Blackfeet.

Nate had a hunch where Traggard would stop for the night, since he had stopped at the same spot several times himself: in a clearing bordered by cottonwoods, where a fire could be kindled safe from hostile eyes. If Nate could get there ahead of them, he could arrange a suitable reception. But the vegetation was thinning, and the dust the bay raised would alert them to his presence.

Nate was content to go on shadowing them.

A blazing red discus was precariously balanced on the rim of the world when Nate came to within a hundred yards of the clearing and reined up. He was close enough now that he should sneak forward on foot, but it was not dark enough. He sat with his back to a cottonwood to await nightfall.

Hector sprawled out next to him, placing his head on Nate's knee.

"Cut that out," Nate said, not used to such affection from beasts.

In its allotted course the sun relinquished its rule of the firmament. Stars glittered like so many fireflies.

"It's time." Nate stood and faced the hound. "Sit," he said, and when Hector obeyed, he added forcefully, "Stay!"

Hector looked up at him with eyes as trusting as a child's.

"Stay!" Nate repeated, gruffly, and padded into the trees. He had his doubts the dog would listen, but when he glanced back Hector was still where he was supposed to be.

"I'll be switched," Nate said, feeling a strange sort of pride in a dog that wasn't even his.

A large moth flitted by. Out on the prairie a coyote barked. Nate had gone only a short way when he had his hunch confirmed. Red and orange flames licked the air in the center of the clearing.

The bounty hunters had stripped their horses and were hunkered around the fire, waiting for a pot of coffee to percolate.

"Do what you want," Sprague was telling the other two, "but I've had enough of these damnable mountains to last me a lifetime. I'm never coming back."

"You'd deprive yourself of your share of the bounty?" Lucian Traggard asked in surprise.

"I'd rather go on breathing, thank you very much."

Nate crawled to within a pebble's toss of where they sat. He sighted down the Hawken and curled his thumb around the hammer. They had a lot to answer for, these three—for Evelyn, for Chases Rabbits, for Jethro Stuart.

It was time to settle accounts.

Chapter Twelve

Nate couldn't do it. He could not bring himself to murder a human being from ambush even when the person deserved it. Certainly Traggard, Jigger, and Sprague had done more than enough to justify his shooting them. Zach would do it, with relish. Shakespeare, in all likelihood, too. Touch the Clouds would not hesitate to count coup on an enemy, whether white or red.

But to coldly kill the three from hiding was a deed Nate's conscience refused to countenance. He lay flat on his stomach, the Hawken's sights centered on Traggard's chest, the hammer cocked. Every fiber in his body screamed for him to do it, to squeeze the trigger.

Instead, Nate slowly rose and stepped into the clearing. Thanks to the mantle of night, they did not spot him right away. He made it halfway to the fire and then Jigger yelped and leaped up while clawing for a pistol. But the small bundle of grime and gristle was not stupid, and at the last instant Jigger opened his fingers wide so Nate could see that he was not going to draw.

"You!" Lucian Traggard exclaimed, likewise heaving to his feet. "You came after us!"

"Did you think I wouldn't?"

Sprague was too flabbergasted to move. He sat with his mouth hanging open, then suddenly flung his arms out from his sides and bawled, "Don't shoot! Don't shoot! In God's name, please don't kill us!"

"You don't like it when the moccasin is on the other foot, do you?" Nate grimly asked. He wished that one of them would resort to a weapon. Any weapon would do—pistol, knife, dagger, anything, just so it gave him an excuse to do what he could not do before.

Tense moments passed, the three at the fire waiting for Nate to blow out their wicks or give some sign of his intentions, and Nate thinking how much easier his life would be if he were more like his son. Zach never had compunctions about killing, from ambush or any other way.

"Well?" Traggard broke the strained silence. "Do we make it easy for you by turning around so you can shoot us in the backs? Or is it your intention to have us stand here until we die of old age?"

Nate squared his shoulders. "One at a time, I want each of you to throw your guns and your blades into the trees as far as you can throw them.

180

No sudden moves, or I send you to the hereafter."

"This life is plenty fine by me," Sprague said, and was the first to relieve himself of his brace of pistols and his knife. "I'd like to live until I'm so old, all my teeth fall out."

Nate trained his Hawken on Jigger. "Your turn."

The rooster offered no argument. To the contrary. "I've got to hand it to you, mountain man. You're as hard to kill as they come. Give me fifty more like you and I could take over these mountains."

Nate gestured at Traggard, who slowly turned in a circle with his arms out to show he had not acquired a weapon since his escape.

"What now?" the tall man in green asked. "Will you line us up and execute us? I think not, or you would have shot us already. Will you let us go? No, you can't do that, either, because you can't risk us coming back to take up where we left off." He chuckled. "What to do? What to do?"

"There are other ways than shooting you," Nate said. He would get to that shortly. Right now he had something more important on his mind. "But I need information first."

Traggard's expression grew wary. "Such as?"

"The name of the lawyer paying the bounty."

"What for? He'll never tell you who his client is. I tried to wheedle it out of him and failed."

"He'll tell me," Nate said. One way or the other. The lawyer was the key to this whole mess.

"And if I won't say? What then? You can't harm a hair on my head or you'll never learn who it is."

"Think again," Nate said, and, drawing a pistol, he cocked it and shot Lucian Traggard in the right thigh.

Howling with pain, Traggard clutched the spurting wound and pitched on his side, his knee bent to his chest. Clenching his teeth, he sputtered and swore and rolled from side to side in a paroxysm of torment.

"The lawyer's name," Nate said.

"Damn you!" Traggard raged. "Damn you to hell! I'll never say! Do you hear me? Never!"

Nate slid the spent flintlock under his belt and drew his other pistol. "You might want to reconsider."

"Look at me!" Traggard's fingers dripped scarlet. "I'm bleeding to death, you bastard!"

"I need to know." Pointing his second pistol at the other leg, Nate thumbed back the hammer.

"Wait! Wait!" Traggard thrust a slick red palm out. "I'm no use to you shot to pieces."

"You're no use at all unless you tell me the lawyer's name," Nate enlightened him. "I'll count to three." He paused, then said quickly, "One. Two. Th—"

"Rufio Praust."

Nate lowered the pistol a few inches. "I've never heard of him. You could be making it up."

"As God is my witness," Traggard said, and crossed himself with his bloody left hand, leaving red smears on his green shirt. "Praust is one of the richest lawyers in New Orleans. Ask anyone who has been there and they're bound to have heard of him."

"The richest?" Nate said. Suddenly, it all made sense—complete, horrible, and fitting sense.

Traggard bobbed his chin, his eyes shut from the agony, blood continuing to seep from under the hand he had over the wound. "He has a plantation outside New Orleans. I've never been there, but I hear his mansion has forty rooms and he owns three hundred slaves. He has two offices, one on the waterfront and another in the heart of the city. He came to Louisiana from Massachusetts about thirty years ago . . ."

Nate was barely listening. He was thinking of Athena Borke, the wealthy woman who had kidnapped Evelyn and was later shot dead. Or so they believed. But what if they were wrong. What if Athena Borke were still alive? She was the one person rich enough, and hate-filled enough, to put a bounty on his family. There was only one way to find out, but it must wait.

Nate focused on the killers. Traggard had stopped talking and they were looking at him expectantly. "Stay right where you are," he cautioned, and went about collecting their horses while keeping the trio covered.

"Hold on!" Sprague cried. "Where are you taking those critters? Without them we wouldn't last a week."

"Have more confidence in yourselves," Nate replied. "I give you ten days until the buzzards feed on your carcasses." He smiled and backed into the vegetation, leading the horses after him, and as soon as the forest swallowed him, he turned and barreled in a beeline toward the bay.

Hector was where Nate had left him, ears pricked, forehead furrowed, as if puzzled by something.

"Did you think I would leave you?" Nate patted the dog's head, then rigged a lead rope for the extra horses. Climbing on the bay, he started south. A whine reminded him he had told the hound to stay. "Heel, boy," he said, and Hector caught up and padded alongside him.

Nate rode a quarter of a mile. Far enough that he doubted the killers would come after him, as dark as it was. He tied the horses, told Hector to stay to guard them, then hurried back to the clearing, crawling the last dozen yards. He made no more noise than a Sioux warrior. As he predicted, they were still there.

Lucian Traggard's thigh had been crudely bandaged. The bleeding had stopped, but Traggard was pasty pale and sweating gallons. Propped on a saddle, he glared at the fire as if the fire were the cause of his misery and not his own greed. "The next time I see that son of a bitch, he's dead!"

Sprague had his arms wrapped around his legs and was rocking on his bottom. "What will we do without horses? We can't make it back to civilization without mounts."

Engrossed in rummaging in a saddlebag, Jigger looked up. "What worries me is why he left us alive." Always the crafty one, he had divined there was more to it than they might think.

"No mystery there," Traggard said. "He's not a man-killer like us. He can't kill in cold blood."

"He could if he had to, I'd warrant," Jigger disagreed. "No, there's more to it."

"Like what?" came from Sprague, who nervously gnawed on his lower lip.

"Like having us die slow and hard."

Sprague snorted. "What does it matter *how* we die? Dead is dead. It seems to me we've got more to worry about than why he didn't kill us outright. Such as how we're going to stay alive without horses."

"It can be done," Jigger said. "If a man has enough grit, he can survive anything life throws at him."

"Listen to you. But you're wrong. All the grit in the world won't stop a man from dying of thirst or hunger. Grit won't deflect the arrows of hostiles. Or cause a hungry grizzly to run us off."

"Just so a man doesn't caterwaul like a baby when his times comes," Jigger said, his nose still in the saddlebag.

"What does that matter?" Sprague snapped. "Here we are stranded on the prairie miles and miles and miles from anywhere, and you hunker there as calmly as if we're at a church social."

Traggard tore his glare from the fire and fixed it on Sprague. "That's enough. All you ever do is bellyache. To hear you gripe, a body would think you were the one who was just shot."

"He gets my goat, is all," Sprague defended himself.

"You don't hear goats complain all the time,"

185

Traggard growled. "Now shut the hell up—or so help me, I'll shut you up." As he said it, his hand drifted to his waist and closed on empty air where his pistol had been.

Still, Sprague was cowed. "Sorry. I don't have a hankering to die, is all."

"Who does?" Traggard retorted. "And none of us is going to if I can help it. At first light, you two hunt for our rifles and pistols and knives. They shouldn't be too hard to find. Then we'll search for mounts. There are bound to be some of those King ran off around somewhere."

"That's right!" Sprague exclaimed. "I had forgotten about them! Or if we had to, we could steal Injun horses." He had transformed into a fount of optimism. "Things aren't so bad. Not really."

The rest of their chatter was small talk. The only comment that interested Nate was a vow Lucian Traggard made shortly before the three of them turned in.

"This isn't over, not by a long shot. I'm coming back with twice as many men and rubbing out Nate King and his entire family, if it's the last thing I ever do."

When Nate was convinced they were asleep, he circled the clearing to where they had tossed their weapons. Carefully groping about in the brush, he found two rifles, a pistol, and a knife. He was about to take them to the horses when he noticed that Sprague had removed his powder horn and ammo pouch and left them on the ground beside him.

Setting down his collection, Nate crept into the

clearing. He would never try something like this with Indians, but these were Easterners, notorious for having senses as dull as blunt plow blades. Tired Easterners, who did not stir an eyelid as he picked up the powder horn and pouch and returned to the forest.

With their weapons once again in hand, Nate hiked south, smiling to himself. They were now at his mercy. Or, rather, at the mercy of that which had no mercy, and the beauty of it was, they did not realize it yet. Maybe Jigger did, since Jigger never missed a thing.

Before first light he was back in the weeds at the edge of the clearing. He had his spyglass and need not get close, but he wanted to hear as well as see, to add to the sweet savor of his revenge. It gave him something to ponder as he waited for them to wake up. He had never thought of himself as an especially vengeful man. But people had a habit of not seeing themselves as they truly were, and he was no different from anyone else.

Jigger woke first. He did not rouse the others but immediately went to the same general area Nate had searched and began hunting for weapons. Although he looked and looked until the sun rose, all he found were a pistol and a knife. The latter he hid under his shirt.

Traggard came awake as Jigger was returning. He blinked and rubbed his eyes, then winced and put both hands on his leg. "Damn. I feel like someone drove a spike into my thighbone. Where have you been?"

187

"I found this," Jigger said, patting the pistol.

"That's all?"

"Go look for yourself," Jigger said. "I made it a point to watch where he threw everything, but the rest of the weapons were gone." He did not tell about the knife under his shirt.

"How can that be?" Traggard demanded.

They looked at each other and both said at the same time, "Nate King."

"So that's how it is!" Lucian Traggard snarled. "He's playing some kind of game with us. He took our horses. He swiped our weapons. You can see where this is leading, can't you?"

"Yes," Jigger said.

"We'll outsmart him. Instead of heading east for the Mississippi, we'll head south to Bent's Fort. On foot it won't take more than a couple of weeks. Or wouldn't, if my leg wasn't so hurt."

Their voices did what the sun had not, and woke Sprague. On hearing the latest development, he stood, anxiety etched clearly on his face. "I want to see for myself. We need more than one measly pistol." He absently touched his shirt, and stiffened. Glancing at the spot where he had left his ammunition pouch and powder horn, he declared, "My bullets and powder are gone! Someone stole them in the middle of the night!"

"Three guesses who," Jigger said.

"We're onto him now, and that makes all the difference," Traggard remarked. "He won't do us in this way. No sir, he won't." Propping his hands under him, he started to rise but sank back down.

"Damn. My leg is next to useless. One of you find me a tree limb I can use as a crutch."

"Sure thing, boss," Sprague dashed to comply.

Jigger draped his saddlebags over his left shoulder. "I hate leaving my saddle for hostiles to find."

Nate did not linger to hear more. Backing away until it was safe to stand, he made his way to the horses and rode west, with his string and the hound keeping pace until he had gone half a mile. In a grassy gully, he drew rein and climbed down. While the horses grazed, he relaxed on his belly on the gully rim and unfolded his spyglass. He did not have long to wait.

In single file they emerged from the green belt bordering the creek and struck off for Bent's Fort. Jigger was in the lead, Sprague next, Traggard hobbled at the rear on a trimmed branch with a fork at the top for his arm.

All that day, the three bounty killers hiked tirelessly south. Nate figured they had stopped at the trading post on their way into the mountains. Bent's was the nearest outpost of any kind, and the only place they were likely to get help. Logically, they were doing the right thing. Rationally, it made complete sense. But it was the worst move they could make.

That night they camped on the open prairie. They kindled a fire, but it did not last long with only grass to burn. The wind picked up, as it invariably did, and the three killers curled up and tried their best to sleep. Only Sprague had brought

189

a blanket; by the brisk hours before dawn, even that would not ward off the chill.

At sunrise they were under way again. Traggard hobbled much more slowly than yesterday, and several times hollered to the others to wait up for him. Through the spyglass, Nate saw Jigger and Sprague frown, and he smiled.

That night was a repeat of the first. Two days now they had gone without water or food.

Nate snuck close to listen.

"It was a mistake to leave the creek," Sprague was complaining. "For all we know, there might not be another for a hundred miles."

"We'll spread out your blanket," Traggard proposed. "In the morning it will be soaked with dew. We'll wring it out and drink enough to last us."

"That will ruin the blanket after a couple of days," Sprague said sullenly.

"Would you rather die of thirst?"

"It's food I'm concerned about," Jigger said. "We haven't come across so much as a lizard and we have no idea which plants are poisonous."

"There have to be rabbits and prairie dogs and such hereabouts," Traggard assured him. "Deer and antelope, too. We'll find something."

The next morning, they eagerly gathered around the blanket and each took a corner to wring. But at that time of year there wasn't much dew. Between them they barely managed a handful. That was not enough for Sprague, who stuck the blanket in his mouth and sucked on it until Traggard barked at him to stop.

A pall of gloom descended as they resumed their trek. Traggard repeatedly had to tell the other two to slow down. The pace Jigger set was much too fast.

At sunset, Nate secreted the horses in a dry wash, told Hector to stay, and once again stalked near enough to eavesdrop. They had a small fire going thanks to buffalo droppings Jigger found. For a long while, no one said anything. Jigger stared into the flames. Sprague had his forehead on his arms. Traggard was on his back, the only way he could make himself comfortable with his leg as swollen as it was.

"We'll never reach Bent's Fort going as slow as we have."

At Jigger's comment, Traggard raised his head and eased onto his side. "I'm doing the best I can."

"That's the problem."

"What are you saying? Spell it out for me so I'm clear what you're thinking."

"I should go on ahead alone. I can go faster, reach the trading post that much sooner. Sprague can stay to lend you a hand."

"Why me stay?" Sprague was quick to speak up. "Why can't I go on ahead and you help him?"

"I have a better chance of making it," Jigger said.

"Like hell. Give me the pistol and I'll have as good a chance as you. I can walk as fast as you. Faster, even, with those short legs you've got."

Traggard gestured sharply. "Quit your arguing. It doesn't matter which of you walks the fastest because we're not splitting up. We're sticking together until we reach Bent's Fort, and that's all there is to it."

"Like hell it is," Jigger said. Drawing his pistol, he shot Lucian Traggard in the head. The slug caught the man in green high in the forehead and blew off the top of his skull, spewing hair and brain and bits of bones and gore every which way. Traggard's eyes rolled up and his body flopped about for five to ten seconds and then was still.

"Sweet Jesus!" Sprague breathed, leaping to his feet. "You killed him! You done went and blew his brains out!"

"He was slowing us down too much," Jigger said, taking hold of his powder horn so he could open it and pour powder into the pistol to reload.

"But you *killed* him!" Sprague screeched. His face was twitching and his arms were jerking.

"I can do you, too, if you don't calm down," Jigger said.

Sprague took a couple of steps back, his eyes wide with stark fear. "You would, too? You'll kill anyone if it suits your purpose." Catching himself, he coiled to spring. "But I'm not going to let you! I'll take that gun from you and then you'll have to do as I say!"

Jigger's right hand disappeared under his shirt and flashed out holding the knife. "You can try."

At that, Sprague wheeled and bolted into the night, shrieking over his shoulder, "You won't get me! No sir! You won't ever get me!"

To Nate's mild surprise, Jigger made no attempt to go after him. The small man sat and listened to the rapidly receding footfalls, and when they faded, he snickered and shook his head. "What an idiot. It's best I'm shed of him. I don't need anyone. I can make it on my own."

Jigger finished reloading and slid the pistol under his belt. Rising, he went to Traggard, stuck a hand in each of the dead man's pockets, and swore. "Nothing. Nothing at all. You're useless in more ways than one." Jigger proceeded to drag the body a goodly distance from the fire.

"This is far enough. The meat eaters shouldn't bother me."

Nate was not the only one who talked to himself when he was alone. Jigger had no sooner sat back down and added another buffalo chip to the flames than he commented, "By my lonesome it shouldn't take more than a week and a half. I can do it. Do it walking in my sleep if I had to."

At daybreak, Nate had a decision to make: to shadow Jigger or Sprague. He decided the coward would keep.

By the middle of the afternoon, Jigger was plodding along like a freight mule after a hard day's haul. Toward evening, he spotted a small herd of buffalo to the southeast. Yanking the pistol out, he ran toward them, eager for a shot, but the wind carried his scent to them and they thundered into the distance before he came within range.

That night Jigger did not bother with a fire. He did spread out the blanket, though, and wrung out the dew the next morning. All he got was another pitiable handful. Then, the blanket looped about his midriff like an oversized belt, he started off strong. But after less than an hour, he was plodding once more, and by noon he was dragging his heels.

Sunset came and went, and still Jigger plodded on. He walked until midnight and collapsed. At first light, he was up. A haggard reflection of his former self, he shuffled steadily southward hour by plodding hour until about noon, when he came to a knoll and walked to the top and plopped down as if his legs had been knocked out from under him.

Through the telescope Nate saw Jigger gaze to the south and Jigger's shoulders slump. The truth was dawning at last. But Nate had to hand it to the little man. Jigger was soon up and on the move again, striding as purposefully, if more wearily, as before.

By nightfall Jigger was walking as one worn to the limits of his endurance. When he stopped, he simply curled into a ball with his chin on his hands.

Darkness rendered the telescope useless. Nate placed it in a parfleche, gave Hector several large pieces of pemmican, and settled in for the night. He slept soundly and was up at his usual time, before the crack of dawn. The spyglass in hand, he waited for the sky to brighten.

But when the crescent of the reborn sun rose, the little man was nowhere to be seen.

Alarmed, Nate climbed on the bay, snatched the lead rope, whistled to the hound, and galloped across the prairie. Footprints were few; the ground was hard, the grass thick.

Nate pointed and gave Hector the command to

track, and they were off, guided by the hound's nose.

Apparently unable to sleep, Jigger had got up sometime during the night and was now miles ahead. Or so Nate thought. But he had ridden only three-quarters of a mile when Hector made a sound that was part growl, part whine, and there, an arrow's flight away, shambled an apparition that resembled nothing so much as a dead man walking.

Jigger did not collapse, though. He did not give up. Nate let the distance between them widen until he was out of pistol range, and followed.

For three and a half more days, Jigger sustained himself on iron will and occasional handfuls of grass. Then his legs did what they inevitably had to do.

When Nate rode up, Jigger was sitting slouched over, weakly tearing at grass and stuffing blades of it in his mouth. Drool dripped down his chin. "You! I knew you were out there somewhere."

Nate leaned on his saddle and did not say anything.

Jigger blinked bloodshot eyes and nodded to the south. "I'm close, aren't I?"

"Not close enough."

"Really? Well, then." Jigger feebly mopped at his mouth with a sleeve. "You think you're clever, don't you? Letting the wilderness do it, so all you have to do is sit back and watch."

"Traggard and you were the clever ones. Too clever by half."

"I curse you, Nate King. I place a curse on you and your family for now and for all time." As he railed, Jigger slid his right hand to his belt. Suddenly, he grabbed at his hip and glanced down.

"Is this what you're looking for?" Nate held up the pistol. "I found it where you slept last night."

"It's not fair," Jigger said bleakly. "I want to kill you for killing me. I want to kill you so much."

Nate lifted his reins. "Your killing days are over."

"Wait!" Jigger tilted his head to regard the circling buzzards. "Don't leave me like this. A sack of bones with blisters on my feet and my legs so cramped, I can't hardly walk."

"You might get another mile."

"Finish it here. One shot is all I ask. A mercy killing. What do you say?"

"Vultures go for the soft parts first. For the eyes, the throat, the stomach. You'll be a long time dying. Your screams will drive them off for a while, but eventually they'll get used to them, and then it's only a matter of time."

"I'll come back to haunt you. So help me God."

Nate smiled, and to the accompaniment of heaped curses, rode out of earshot and made camp. He slept well. The next morning, he dallied over a breakfast of coffee and jerky. He did not need the hound to track for him. A dark roiling cloud of feathered scavengers marked the spot. As he predicted, Jigger had lasted another mile. And as he had warned, the buzzards had gone for the soft parts first.

The ride north was uneventful.

Sprague had made it as far as the creek and the clearing. That was where a band of warriors found him. Arapahos, judging by a broken arrow. Sometimes the Arapahos were friendly. Sometimes they weren't. These hadn't been. They had riddled Sprague with arrows but pulled the arrows out since arrows were hard to come by. They also lifted Sprague's hair.

In the bright rosy light of a clear day, Nate King gigged his mount toward the emerald foothills. He had to return a certain hound and rejoin his family and friends. Then it was on to their new home deep in the mountains, and his date with a certain grizzly.

#45
WILDERNESS
IN CRUEL CLUTCHES
David Thompson

Zach King, son of legendary mountain man Nate King, is at home in the harshest terrain of the Rockies. But nothing can prepare him for the perils of civilization. Locked in a deadly game of cat-and-mouse with his sister's kidnapper, Zach wends his way through the streets of New Orleans like the seasoned hunter he is. Yet this is not the wild, and the trappings of society offer his prey only more places to hide. Dodging fists, knives, bullets and even jail, Zach will have to adjust to his new territory quickly—his sister's life depends on it.

RIDERS TO MOON ROCK

ANDREW J. FENADY

Like the stony peak of Moon Rock, Shannon knew what it was to be beaten by the elements yet stand tall and proud despite numerous storms. Shannon never quite fit in with the rest of the world. First raised by Kiowas and then taken in by a wealthy rancher, he found himself rejected by society time after time. Everything he ever wanted was always just out of his grasp, kept away by those who resented his upbringing and feared his ambition. But Shannon is determined to wait out his enemies and take what is rightfully his—no matter what the cost.

LOREN ZANE GREY
AMBUSH FOR LASSITER

Framed for a murder they didn't commit, Lassiter and his best pal Borling are looking at twenty-five years of hard time in the most notorious prison of the West. In a daring move, they make a break for freedom—only to be double-crossed at the last minute. Lassiter ends up in solitary confinement, but Borling takes a bullet to the back. When at last Lassiter makes it out, there's only one thing on his mind: vengeance.

ZANE GREY
RANGLE RIVER

No name evokes the excitement and glory of the American West more than Zane Grey. His classic *Riders of the Purple Sage* is perhaps the most beloved novel of the West ever written, and his short fiction has been read and cherished for nearly a century. The stories collected here for the first time in paperback are among his very best. Included in this volume are two short novels and two short stories, plus two firsthand accounts of Grey's own early adventures in the territories that he so notably made his own. Zane Grey was an author who experienced the living West and wrote about it with a clarity and immediacy that touches us to this day.
